DESTRUCTION

BAND OF BELIEVERS, BOOK 3

JAMIE LEE GREY

Copyright © 2018 by Jamie Lee Grey

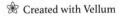 Created with Vellum

To Mom,
For everything.
I love you very much!

And to my nieces and nephews...
May you be called, chosen and committed!

CONTENTS

1

Something moved in the darkening Montana sky, and eighteen-year-old <u>Willow Archer</u> cast an anxious glance upward, hoping to see an owl or a bat winging its way through the deepening twilight. Could the government agents have gotten their drones working? Were they, even now, peering at her as she walked back from the outhouse to the little one-room cabin? Was her group in danger again? So soon?

She froze, straining to find the source of the movement.

The brightest stars twinkled in the sky's blue velvet canvas. The moon had not yet risen. Willow scanned the celestial space slowly, then finally spotted it – one star was moving across the sky. But was it a star? Or a satellite?

Could it be an airplane? Was someone flying a jet in the United States? Maybe they were coming from a region that hadn't been hit by the EMP?

No, it wasn't a plane. Too high, too far away, wrong speed.

She exhaled slowly. Well, nothing to fear from a satellite. Not yet, anyway. Even if the government wanted to find Christians by satellite surveillance, they'd have to have functioning electronics on the ground in order to see any of the data from the satellites. And that wasn't too likely, given the recent EMP.

On the other hand, maybe re-established satellite surveillance wasn't too far off, given that the City of Ponderosa obviously had gotten some electricity back online. And running water, as well. Who knew how the rest of the country was faring?

She started back toward the cabin, the breeze blowing her long auburn locks across her face. Satellites and drones might be worries for a future day. For now, she just needed to keep her group safe, alive and fed.

Someone had propped open the cabin door with a large rock. She couldn't blame them. July was turning hot and muggy. All those bodies in the cabin made it feel like a slow cooker. The ancient window only opened about an inch before it got stuck against its warped wooden frame. Matt and Josh were up in the loft, while Raven snored like a baby bear on one of the top bunks at the rear of the cabin. Candy and little Maria appeared to be sleeping soundly on the lower bunk beds.

The breeze blew, fanning fresh air across Willow's skin as she paused in the doorway. They'd all sleep better with the ventilation. But an open door was an invitation to bears.

She shuddered. The scars on her leg from the grizzly attack were still bright and fresh. The sow's roar thundered through her memory. The beady eyes, the snapping jaws, the agony of those huge claws shredding her flesh... she winced.

Her hand trembled as she pulled the door shut and latched it. She took off her boots, then climbed into the bunk above Maria. Except for the toddler, most of the group had given up the luxury of removing clothing before going to bed. One never knew when the next crisis would strike, and if it struck in the middle of the night, nobody wanted to waste time pulling on their pants.

She wadded up Mom's sweater under her head and once

again wished for a real pillow. That was another luxury that had been given up when they'd fled civilization. If she ever had another chance though, she'd get one... a nice, big, fluffy white pillow with a cool cotton pillowcase.

Lying on top of her sleeping bag, she closed her eyes. She was tired, so very tired. But she was also hot. The air was stifling, even with the window cracked open.

She flopped onto her side. The odds of a bear coming to the cabin were slim, she knew. The odds of a second attack seemed minuscule.

Her discomfort fought with her fear and finally won out. She slipped to the floor, padded to the door in her stocking feet, and opened it.

A blessed blast of fresh mountain air cooled her sweaty face. She was just turning around to return to her bunk when her peripheral vision caught motion in the night sky. She scurried outside.

A blazing star streaked across the dark sky, then burned out.

A meteor! Willow smiled. A wishing star.

What should she wish for? Mom. She wished that somehow, she could find Mom. Or even get news of her. Since she'd been detained in the church roundup in Missoula, there had been no news. And that had been before the EMP. Was she still captive? Was she still alive?

A second star blazed across the sky, this one brighter than the last. So she could make a second wish.

What about Jacob? She frowned. Since he'd disappeared after the gunfight, they'd found no trace of him. She truly did not believe he'd been injured. Had he abandoned them? Betrayed them?

Should she wish that he'd be found alive? Or that he'd be found dead?

A third star flashed a blazing trail, then flickered out.

This was a regular meteor shower! She should awaken the others, so they could watch. She hurried inside, shook Raven awake, then left her to tell Candy while Willow climbed the ladder to the loft. Grabbing Josh's ankle, she gave a good tug.

"Wha –" Josh yanked his foot away.

"Wake up! There's a meteor shower!" Willow shook Matt's ankle the same way. "Wake up! Shooting stars!"

Matt sat up. Willow climbed down the ladder and walked outside. Raven and Candy had already come out, and were gawking at a meteor. Then two blazed off at once.

"Look at that!" Candy enthused. "This is great!"

The boys stumbled out the door. They stared at the heavens.

"Did we miss it all?" Matt asked.

"I doubt it," Raven said. "Just give it a minute."

Josh flopped to the ground, then settled on his back, eyes to the sky. "I see one!"

Matt gave a low whistle as the meteor flashed to its death. "Awesome!"

Suddenly, the sky began to brighten.

"What on earth?" Candy's tone mixed amazement and fear.

A ball of brilliant light blazed overhead, illuminating the cabin, the clearing and the mountains beyond as if it were mid-day. It was like looking at the sun. As it grew nearer and brighter, Willow covered her eyes. And then it was gone.

She opened her eyes, but couldn't see a thing. Slowly, they started to adjust.

"Whoa." Josh sat up. "That was crazy."

BOOM! BOOM! BOOM!

The shockwave felt like an earthquake, but sounded like a bomb explosion.

Willow clapped her hands to her ears. The cabin shook, its windows rattling precariously in their frames.

Inside the cabin, Maria screamed. Candy rushed through

the door to her daughter. Gilligan rushed out, barking.

Booms like thunder continued filling the air. Finally, the noise tapered off.

Ears ringing, Willow struggled to refocus in the dark night.

Candy carried her wailing toddler outside. "What should we do?"

Willow laughed. "You mean to hide from meteorites?"

"We should pray," Raven suggested.

She was right. As more meteors ripped open the sky, the group held an impromptu prayer vigil. Everyone kept their eyes open.

Only one more meteorite came as close as the first one. This one appeared much smaller, though, and they actually saw where it landed.

THE HOUSE SHOOK and threw Jacob Myers out of bed. He scrambled in the darkness, untangling his feet from the blankets. Glass shattered and tinkled on the hard floor.

What in the world? Where was he?

Concussive bombs were going off. It sounded like a war zone.

He leapt up, slicing his bare foot on the broken glass.

Yelping, he loosed an expletive and grabbed his foot. Then he remembered. He was at Marcus Laramie's house in Ponderosa, Montana. There had been an EMP. How could the country be at war? Maybe they were under attack, but they couldn't be fighting back. They weren't able to.

The explosions and concussions died down. Their noise was replaced by the barking of about a dozen dogs. Little yappy yelps, big ferocious woofs, and a cacophony of canine voices in between.

He'd been sleeping on the sofa. And he remembered putting a flashlight on the coffee table, within reach.

Feeling around on the floor, he found several shards of glass, and finally, the flashlight. He flicked it on.

The window had been blown out by the blast, shattering and throwing huge shards of glass down on the sofa where he'd been sleeping moments before. It might have killed him, if he hadn't been thrown off the sofa at the same time

His pants were where he'd left them, on a chair across the room, and his boots were on the floor beside the chair. He hobbled over to them, watching for glass as he took each step.

"Marcus?" He yelled. "You okay?"

"I'm outside." The answer drifted through the broken window. "C'mon out!"

The cut on his foot didn't look too terrible, so Jacob shook out his clothes and boots, dressed, grabbed his Glock, and hurried out the front door.

"What's going on?"

He flashed the light on Marcus, who sat on a lawn chair in the middle of the yard. The guy turned, then shielded his eyes from the light.

"Get that out of my eyes!"

Jacob lowered the flashlight.

"What are you doing out here?"

Marcus spat in the grass. "Watching the meteors, obviously. Just had a real fine one."

"That? It wasn't an earthquake?"

"Nah. Impressive, wasn't it? I almost fell out of my chair."

"It busted your window."

Marcus turned, looked and cursed.

The next door neighbor, about the age of Jacob's grandmother, came screaming out of her house in her bathrobe and slippers.

"War! We're at war!" Her shrill voice reached a high-pitched shriek. She looked toward Marcus. "Do you have a bomb shelter?"

"We're not at war, Mrs. Dennison," Marcus assured her. "Calm down. It's a meteor shower."

"Are you crazy? Meteor showers don't explode like bombs!"

"We had a close meteorite. If you go back inside, stay away from your windows." His voice was calm, maybe from his years of working crises as a police officer. He seemed unflappable. Jacob had to give the guy credit for that. He lowered himself to the grass beside Marcus' chair.

"I cut my foot."

"How bad is it?"

"Not too bad, I guess. About an inch long, but superficial."

"When this show blows over, we'll have to clean it up. Don't want an infection getting started there."

Jacob stretched out on the lawn. The barking and yapping wound down as the neighbors gathered their dogs and spoke excitedly over their fences. Overhead, a distant meteor streaked, then faded away.

Eventually, the neighborhood quieted. Jacob yawned.

His eyes grew tired and finally closed.

Next thing he knew, it was morning. He sat up and pushed off a quilt. The top was covered with dew. Marcus must have thrown it over him during the night. Despite his gruff exterior, he was a decent guy. And calm under pressure.

Jacob shook out the quilt and hung it over the deck railing to dry. He walked into the house. Marcus wasn't in the kitchen or the living room. Maybe he was gone. Or still asleep.

The living room was a mess. In the light of day, it was apparent how close he'd come to death last night. The sofa where he'd been sleeping was directly under a large window, maybe five feet tall and eight feet wide. The shock wave had shattered the glass, blowing shards into the room and dropping huge jagged pieces onto the sofa, where they pierced the fabric like shrapnel. Now they stood there like jagged mountain peaks protruding from the cloth.

Jacob pulled a piece out of the sofa. It was buried deep in the cushion with its deadly sharp points.

How had he survived this?

He'd been thrown off the sofa, sure, but wouldn't that have been in the same instant as the glass shattered and fell? He must have been tossed out a moment earlier.

Maybe one moment had seen him tossed and the glass break, and the next had seen him hit the floor as the glass hit the sofa.

He swallowed. A single moment had saved his life.

"Good! You're awake." Marcus's voice boomed from the hall. "Let's get this mess cleaned up."

UNCLE TONY RUBBED the sleep from his tired eyes and stretched. He'd overslept. No surprise, given that he'd been up half the night with all the celestial excitement.

He had been about a mile from town, on his way to get a crowbar from his niece's house, when the meteors started blazing. Eventually, he'd decided to crash at her place for the night. She was gone, but she wouldn't mind. Raven would never come back here. It was too dangerous for Christians in town.

Which was why he needed to get up and get out of here. He swung his feet off the bed, pulled on his boots, then reached for his pack.

As he headed toward the hall, he caught his reflection in the mirror. He looked away quickly, but not before he noticed his red-lined eyes, scruffy grey beard and even scruffier hair. He looked like a true homeless scoundrel.

Which wasn't too far from the truth. But he'd lived like a mountain man for years. He preferred the world as God had made it: natural, beautiful and peaceful. Society had just made a noisy mess. And it had gotten worse with each passing year.

Before he headed back to the forest, he had to make a pit stop. So he dropped his pack in the hall and went into the bath room. After he finished his business there, he looked through the cabinet and the linen closet. Most everything useful had already been looted. He averted his gaze from the mirror over the sink. Didn't need another reminder about his age or appearance.

Back in the hall, he shouldered his pack, then headed for the living room. Through the window there, he saw two men approaching the house from the road.

More looters?

He should run them off. Just because Raven wasn't coming back, didn't give criminals the right to rifle through her house. It belonged to her!

They were coming through the yard as he reached the front door. Before he yanked it open, he checked through the window to see how well armed they might be. Didn't need to get killed over this.

Wait! The first man was his estranged nephew, Marcus, who was a police captain. And that was Jacob Myers with him!

Stunned, Tony drew back from the door. How did those two know each other, and why were they coming to Raven's house? Looking for her? Did they think she'd come home? Marcus had been chasing Raven and her Christian friends to make them take the Mark.

He spun and headed for the back door. He'd figure this all out later. If he could get out of here before they caught him.

2

The sun toasted her head as <u>Willow</u> weeded the carrot row by hand, careful to not disturb a single baby carrot. They couldn't afford to lose any future food. Behind her, Deborah Wilcox and her daughter Jaci Collins weeded the potatoes.

Willow stood and stretched her back. Beyond the garden, Deborah's granddaughter Beth babysat Maria in the shade of an old lodgepole pine. The boys and the rest of Deborah's family were working on the new Collins cabin, while Candy was cleaning up from lunch.

It seemed good that the Wilcox/Collins family had decided not to move to John Anderson's retreat. She was sure it'd been a tough decision. The retreat had been well planned, and it had everything – stored food, solar power, propane appliances, running water from a spring on the hill above the house, and livestock including milk cows, horses and chickens.

She glanced at her own chickens, happily scratching at the ground in their portable pen. They were producing eggs, which provided the group with some valuable protein.

But the Andersons' place had one big problem – it was on

the road system. A narrow, bumpy one-lane Forest Service road, but it was still accessible by vehicle. That made it easy to find. And vulnerable, as they'd all recently experienced.

"Halloo the house!"

Willow started at the man's voice from the forest. But she calmed herself as she recognized it.

Raven's uncle Tony emerged from the trees. Where was Raven, anyway? Helping with the new cabin?

Willow started toward Tony. As she closed the distance, she quickened her pace. He didn't look good. His red face shone with sweat under his beat-up hat. He leaned on his walking stick with every hurried step. His breath came in gasps.

"Tony!" She reached a hand out toward him. "Are you alright?"

He shook his head. "Water."

She turned and ran back to the cabin, filled a mug with filtered water, and raced back to him. The others were beginning to gather around.

"Raven?" Tony wheezed.

"Does anyone know where Raven is?" Willow looked from one person to the next.

"I think she went to the creek," Candy said. "To haul water."

"Go get her," Willow urged. When Candy hesitated, she ordered, "Now!"

Candy scurried toward the creek, and Willow turned back to Tony. "Let's get you into the shade. You might be getting heat stroke."

She led him to a large pine tree.

"Here, sit down. Are you feeling okay?"

Tony sat, and sipped the water slowly. Finally, he looked up.

"I have news." He handed the empty mug to her. "Thanks."

"What news?" She handed the mug to Jaci. "Would you please go fill that again?"

Deborah touched her daughter's elbow. "And bring some salt back with you, too."

"Okay." Jaci's eyebrows rose, but she headed toward the cabin.

"I'll tell you all when Raven gets here." Uncle Tony leaned back against the tree trunk and shut his eyes.

Willow turned to Beth, who was holding Maria on her hip.

"I'll keep an eye on Maria. I need you to run as fast as you can up to your family's new cabin, and get your dad and everyone else. Tell them Tony is here, and he has news."

"Alright." The girl set the child down, then raced up the hill toward the new cabin site.

She returned with the building group about the same time Candy returned with Raven. Jaci handed a full mug of water to Tony, and Deborah encouraged him to eat some salt.

"I think you need to replenish your electrolytes," she explained.

He nodded, ate a little salt, and washed it down with water. His breathing had finally slowed to normal. But his face still looked red.

Raven sat beside him.

"Are you okay?" She studied her uncle. "What's going on?"

"Don't worry about me. It's Jacob you need to worry about. Him and Marcus."

"What?" Willow plunked herself down directly in front of the visitor. "Why?"

"I'll start at the beginning." Uncle Tony drew a long breath, then released it. "I was close to town last night when the meteors started going. I needed a crowbar, and I thought there might be one in Raven's garden shed. I checked, but pretty much every-thing has been stolen already. After watching the sky for a long time, I got tired and decided to stay the night there."

He turned his watery eyes on his niece. "Hope you

don't mind."

"Of course not!" She gripped his shoulder. "You're always welcome. Wherever I might live."

Her dark brown eyes turned toward the cabin and clearing as she fingered her long black braid. "Tell us the rest."

"I slept in. But God woke me up before it got too late, or I would've really been in trouble."

"How?" Willow asked.

"Why?" Candy pressed, her blonde curls framing her bright blue eyes. "What happened?"

"Well, He just made sure I woke up before – but I'm getting ahead of myself. On my way out, I checked for any helpful supplies in the bathroom, but all the good stuff was taken." He looked at his niece. "Sorry, Raven. They really went through your place."

"It's okay." She shrugged. "It's just stuff, right?"

"It's wrong, is what it is!" Uncle Tony coughed and took another sip of water. "So there I was, getting ready to leave, and I saw two looters coming toward the house. I headed toward the front door to run them off."

"Oh, no." Candy pressed her fingers against her mouth.

"Yep. But I stopped to look out the little window in the front door – you know, to make sure I wasn't going to be outgunned – and I recognized them."

"Marcus and Jacob?" Willow could hardly believe it. What did those two have to do with each other? And why were they going to Raven's house?

"You got it."

"Are you sure? You got a real clear look at them?" Raven leaned forward and studied her uncle's eyes. "I mean, is there any way – are you positive?"

"My eyes are fine. It's my heart that gives me trouble."

"What?" Raven's eyes widened. "You have heart trouble?

Since when?"

"Since I became an old man. But that's a separate problem. Focus!" He looked at Raven and Willow, then at their friends gathered in the shade of the old pine. "You guys have a real problem here!"

"That's for sure," Willow agreed. "But finish your story. Did you hear anything? What else did you see? And how did you get away?"

"Well, when I saw it was those two scoundrels, I hurried my feet right out the back door! They were coming up the front walk, and I have no doubt they let themselves in. In fact, as I skedaddled past the garden shed, I heard the screen door bang shut."

He picked up a pine cone and studied it.

"Anyway, I hurried up to let you know." He looked at his niece. "You're all at risk now. Jacob knows about the group, and the retreat, and the cabin. He can lead Marcus right to you. And those two looked pretty chummy. Like best buds for years, if you know what I mean."

"But why?" Candy's eyes watered like she was going to cry. "Why would Jacob do that? He likes us."

"Maybe he used us," Willow answered. "It's easier to survive in a group, than to survive solo."

Candy hung her head. "I just can't believe it."

"Well, you better start," Raven retorted. "It happened, and we're exposed. Now we have to figure out what to do."

Willow studied the faces of the new family. Alan, the patriarch, looked calm, his hazel eyes steadily focused on Uncle Tony. Beside him, Deborah clutched his hand, concern etched in the lines of her forehead.

Their daughter Jaci was planted firmly beside her husband, Clark, her arms crossed and eyes downcast. Clark's dark eyes blazed – maybe in fury, maybe in defiance – Willow couldn't be sure. Their daughters, Beth and Delia, moved closer to their parents.

Candy scooped up little Maria. "We need to get out of here. They might be on their way, right now!"

"Maybe we should go take them out," Josh blurted.

"Joshua Michael Archer!" Willow glared at her brother.

"Before they get us," he added.

"We can't go around murdering people." Willow glanced around the group. Clark's jaw tightened, but Alan finally spoke up.

"Willow is right. We can't hunt down people because we think they might be out to get us."

"Oh, Marcus is out to get us. For sure." Raven looked at Alan. "I know. He's family."

"It is true." Clark's accent kicked in. "I was there, in the market, the last time."

"But Jacob?" Candy asked. "He's always helped us."

"Why are you always defending him?" Raven's voice grew uncharacteristically sharp. "He's in cahoots with Marcus! You know, the guy who chased us all over these mountains?"

Finally, Matt broke his silence.

"Don't forget. He left me captive when he escaped."

"But he went back to help rescue you, too," Willow pointed out.

"Now *you're* defending him?" Raven's eyes accused her friend.

"No. I've never trusted him. You, of all people, know that!"

What was up with Raven, anyway? Willow studied her best friend. It wasn't like her to be hostile. Raven refused to meet her gaze. Willow sighed. They would need to talk about this later.

Tony lifted his hand to get the group's attention.

"After I got away from Raven's house, when I got to the woods, I stopped and reconsidered. I thought about taking those two out. It's wrong, I know, and I've never killed a man, but I figured I'd be protecting the whole lot of you. Like self-defense in advance."

When no one responded, he continued.

"If Jacob brings Marcus and his team up here, you're all doomed. But if you run before he arrives, you probably won't be able to survive the winter."

He pointed at the garden. "You can't take that with you."

Willow knew it was true. The garden, which might produce enough to help them survive, could not be picked up and moved. The group would face starvation.

"Our cabin is nearly completed," Clark stated. "We cannot move that, either. If we leave here, what will we live in, when winter comes? Tents?"

Willow frowned. He was right, of course. His family's new cabin was well underway, and the old cabin provided shelter for Willow's original group. Plus, there was the barn for the animals. Which Jacob, ironically, had helped renovate. He had also worked on the new cabin, so he knew exactly where it was located, too.

She looked at the friends surrounding her. And realized, again, it was all her fault. Her disobedience weeks ago had resulted in Jacob arriving at the cabin and meeting her group in the first place. One wrong decision, which seemed like a noble one at the time – to try to find her friends and brother – had exposed them all to great danger.

She'd heard that still, soft voice telling her to remain home, to not search that day. God was obviously bringing them home safely already. But she'd bullheadedly taken matters into her own hands. It was such a small, seemingly good and inconsequential decision.

And now, look at this. What a mess! Would they all die because of her sin?

Willow cleared her throat and rose to her feet. Eyes turned expectantly toward her.

"We need to pray. All of us. Together and separately, about what to do."

Alan and Deborah nodded. Clark dropped his gaze, but Willow noticed his shoulders relax in a hint of acquiescence.

"Alan." As his eyes met hers, Willow asked, "Would you please lead us in prayer?"

He nodded and squeezed Deborah's hand. Their younger granddaughter, Beth, reached for his free hand. He bowed his head. The group did the same.

As he began praying, Willow could barely focus on the words. Her heart heavy, she wanted to run to the forest for a good cry. Hadn't she already repented for her disobedience? And yet, it had brought this great trouble to her friends and family. Maybe she should leave the group, strike out on her own, so her actions wouldn't affect them anymore.

Like Jonah. It's my fault, throw me overboard! Jonah had been swallowed by a huge fish. And worse, he'd survived in there for days. *Oh, puke and disgusting!*

She forced her mind back to Alan's prayer just as he finished. "Amen."

"We will need to have someone standing guard at all times, from now on," Willow said. "We'll set up a schedule for that. Everyone will take turns."

Her gaze swept the group. "I guess we should let the Andersons know about this as soon as possible. They'll need to make some decisions, as well."

She paused. "Any volunteers to make the trip over there?"

Delia raised her hand. "I'll go."

"I'll go, too," Matt volunteered.

Willow blinked. Were those two sweet on each other? Maybe. Matt and Josh had been thrilled when the Collins family with their young beauties joined the group. And they were all close in age. Matt was 15, Delia was 14, the same age as Josh, while Beth was 12.

Neither Clark nor Jaci objected, so Willow agreed. After all, these teenagers were practically adults in this crazy new world – they faced the same dangers and shouldered nearly equal responsibilities.

"Alright. Take ammo and water, and be back by dinner." They'd have to hustle to get there, deliver their news, and return by dinner. And that was good. They wouldn't have time to get into trouble. "And be sure to ask if they have any thoughts or suggestions we haven't considered."

The pair took off to prepare for their hike, and Raven stood and offered a hand to her uncle.

"You should stay a while and relax," she said. "And tell me about your heart."

"Nothing to worry about." He allowed her to pull him to his feet. "I'm just old and decrepit."

"You're 58," she said matter-of-factly.

"Exactly. Old." He winked at her. "I think I'll use that excuse to take the afternoon off. It was a hot hike up here from town."

"Why don't you take a nap in the cabin?" Raven asked. "We've got those bunks."

Uncle Tony gazed around at the woods and sky. "Better yet, I think I'll take a nap by the creek. Nice and cool and shady."

He headed off, and Willow caught Raven's eye.

"Got a minute?" Willow asked.

Raven shrugged. "Sure."

Willow steered her away from the group.

"What's going on? Your fuse seems short."

"What do you mean? When?"

"Mostly toward Candy, but also to me."

"Jacob is bad news. And now he's betraying us to Marcus! You were both defending him. What were you thinking?"

Willow bristled. "I was not defending him. I was just pointing out that his actions, while he was here, were reasonable."

"He tricked us." Raven's sweet face darkened into a frown. "Now he's working with my half-brother. What if he was working with Marcus all along? What if Marcus sent him to infiltrate our group, then bring back intel so they could capture us?"

"There's nothing we can do about that now."

Tears sparked in Raven's dark eyes. "It's my fault."

"No." Willow knew exactly whose fault it was, and it wasn't Raven's. "It's not."

"It is! Marcus is only after us because he gave me a personal warning, and I blabbed it to the world." She swiped at her eyes. "Nobody listened, anyway."

"We listened."

"What, five people? I tried to warn hundreds!"

"What they did with that is on them. You did the right

thing." Willow laid her hand on her friend's shoulder. "And you can't be blamed for anything that Marcus or Jacob does."

Raven's eyes searched Willow's, then shifted toward the cabin. She sighed.

"I hope you're right."

"I am."

Raven turned toward the barn. "I should water the chickens."

As Raven walked away, Willow reconsidered her words to Raven. She wondered if they applied to her, as well. Maybe she didn't bear the blame for what Marcus and Jacob were doing. Maybe her sins really were covered after she repented from them.

There was a difference, though, because Raven's issue was not a sin. She had done right. Willow had done wrong.

A whiff of smoke floated past her nose, then was gone. She glanced toward the cabin. No smoke rose from the chimney. Had someone started a camp fire nearby? In the middle of a hot day?

She inhaled slowly, but didn't smell any more smoke. Perhaps she'd imagined it.

That evening, Delia and Matt returned breathlessly to the cabin just as the group was gathering for dinner. Their daypacks were bulging.

"We brought goodies!" Delia's brown eyes danced with her pristine smile. "From the Andersons."

The pair slipped off their packs and began producing surprises.

"Hard candy!" Matt raised a bag of Christmas candy high above his head.

"And fudge!" Delia triumphantly lifted a carefully-wrapped package. "Mrs. Anderson made it yesterday!"

"You better not have eaten any on the way home!" Beth admonished her older sister. "I know how you are."

"We didn't eat anything on the way home." Matt winked at Delia.

"But they did feed us a little while we were there." Delia rubbed her stomach. "Mashed potatoes and gravy!"

"I'm going next time!" Beth pouted.

The girls' father laid his hand on Delia's shoulder.

"Did they have any ideas or suggestions for us?"

"No." Her black curls swung around her shoulders as she looked at Clark. "They thanked us for bringing them the news as soon as we found out, though."

"They had concerns of their own," Matt said. "When we got there, they were making plans for evacuating."

"Why?" Willow asked.

"They said there's a fire on the ridge south of their property. It's a few miles away, but we saw the smoke."

"And we could smell it." Delia wrinkled her nose. "They aren't sure they'll evacuate, though. They're just getting ready. Just in case."

"Do they need help?" Clark asked.

"I don't know." Delia looked at Matt. "We should have asked."

For the first time, Willow regretted not sending someone older to the Andersons. An adult might have gotten better information.

"Where will they go?" She asked.

"They aren't sure." Matt raked his fingers through his overgrown blond hair. "They said it depends on wind direction and speed and... something else."

"They might head down the road toward the highway," Delia said. "The other options are east, deeper into the forest, which might burn up. Or north, to us. But they won't do that if the winds are from the south, like they are now."

"They think a meteorite started the fire," Matt said. "John

went to check it out, but it was already a couple acres, growing fast and real hot in the underbrush. Too big to fight, without real fire crews and water drops from helicopters."

Uncle Tony scratched his cheek. "Fires have always been a big problem here, but now things will be out of control. All anybody'll be able to do is run. If they can."

"The Andersons have that gravity-fed water system, so they're planning to put sprinklers on the house and barn if they have to leave," Matt said. "They think they might run out of water, but maybe they can save the structures. They're afraid they could lose everything though, which is one reason they sent us home with this food."

"I've got a twenty-pound bag of white rice." Delia hefted it from her pack.

"And I've got twenty pounds of dry beans," Matt added.

In spite of the crisis, a moment of joy rushed through Willow and she wanted to jump and holler. Forty pounds of rice and beans!

"Fantastic!" She grinned. "Rice and beans together form a complete protein. It will fill our bellies and provide lots of energy. That was so kind of John and Jeannie! We should pack that up for this winter, when we really need it."

"You might be needing it soon, if you have to run," Uncle Tony said. "If that fire hits the top of John Anderson's ridge, you should see it from here, and you should head out. If it's moving fast, you won't have much time."

"That's quite a ways from here," Deborah pointed out. "A few miles, right? Maybe three or four?"

"Sure. But fires can run fast. Especially if it's windy. But even if it's not, big fires will create their own wind. It might take days, or it could be here in an hour or less."

Uncle Tony paused, his watery eyes moving from one person to the next. "And don't forget, those big forest fires explode and throw flaming material way out ahead of them, and they start new fires in front of the big blaze."

"Have you ever been near a big fire, Uncle Tony?" Raven's dark eyes studied her uncle.

"No way, I stay far away from wildfires. But growing up, my mom always talked about the Sundance Fire in northern Idaho. She lived there at the time, and said that fire went crazy. The forest was so hot and dry, it exploded into flames in front of the fire. I expect that was because of the flaming debris the fire shot out in front of it. Anyway, they got bad winds and the fire ran sixteen miles in nine hours. It created a fire storm that fueled winds that snapped off huge trees. It was so hot, it split huge granite boulders." Tony looked at his niece. "Now, that was some fire!"

"Whoa." Josh's eyes were round.

"Crazy," Matt agreed.

"We've gotta get out of here," Candy said. "First Jacob and Marcus, and now wildfire! What are we waiting for?"

"We're waiting for God," Willow answered. "If He leads us to leave, we will go. Otherwise, we're staying put. Plus, where would we go?"

"But isn't this a sign?" Candy asked. "I mean, we prayed earlier for God to give us some direction, and now we're hearing about an out of control wild fire. That seems like direction, to me!"

Her blue eyes turned imploringly on Alan and Deborah. "By itself, the Jacob thing is pretty scary, and now it's like God is sending us another reason to get out of here. Because we didn't figure it out earlier, from the Jacob and Marcus news."

"They aren't necessarily related." Alan's hazel eyes were calm. "And that fire does not seem to be a direct threat to us. It might not even be a direct threat to the Andersons."

"But it's wise of them to prepare," Deborah added. "Since it's not too far from their home."

Willow found herself sniffing the air, searching for a smoky scent. But all she smelled was the dinner, fast growing cold.

"We should pray and eat," she said. "Clark, would you ask the blessing?"

AFTER DINNER, she studied the horizon to the south. There was a faint haze. It might be smoke, but it was hard to tell. She and Raven washed dishes, talking quietly as they worked.

"Do you think the Lord will move us?" Raven asked.

"Not yet." Willow dried a plate. "What about you? Have you heard anything?"

"Nothing definite. Sometimes I don't hear Him too well, though."

"Yeah, that's a problem. Wouldn't it be great if we could hear perfectly, all the time?"

"Yes." Raven washed the last spoon. "One day, we will. In the meantime, we just have to listen and do our best."

"To be honest, I don't want to leave," Willow whispered, glancing around to see if anyone was near enough to hear their conversation. "Where would we go?"

"That's a big problem. I think the Lord brought us here. Plus, there's the garden...."

Willow sighed. "And we're trying to get things together to survive the winter. Cabins, barn, food storage. We need to start on firewood, too."

Raven burst into a laugh. "Maybe let's wait on that, until after the threat of wildfire is past."

"Yeah," Willow smiled. "I guess that can wait."

Uncle Tony walked over to them, a strange look on his face. His voice was low when he spoke.

"I've been watching the horizon. My eyes are old, but... is that a plume I see?" He pointed toward the Anderson retreat.

It was difficult to make out, but somewhere beyond the Andersons' ridge, it did look like a slim plume of blue-grey smoke was rising into the evening sky.

Willow sucked in her breath. That wildfire was growing.

4

L aura Archer climbed out of the dry culvert where she'd spent the hot July afternoon napping. Her shoes – the ones she'd worn to church that fateful Sunday – had blistered her heels. They weren't designed for walking distances, much less hiking. But at least they were flats, instead of heels. And they were leather, which had been kinder to her feet over the length of the trek.

Her stomach growled as a soft breeze blew cooler air through the Montana mountains. It'd been a day since her last meal. Maybe she could scrounge something tonight. Cattail roots were getting old.

She walked along the shoulder of the highway, following it north. Always north toward Ponderosa. Her children, Willow and Josh, were there, and she would find them.

They might not be at home. Very likely they'd left. The last message – the only one she'd been able to send them – had been a cryptic warning to head for the hills. She hoped they'd gotten the message and done that, and spared themselves the grief she'd suffered.

It had been terrible. Psychological torture first, then physical.

How many had given in, and taken the mark? Only five had still been in captivity with her when she escaped. What had happened to the others? Had they died at the agents' hands, or had they accepted the chip?

She would never know. All she knew now was, she needed to get home. Find her family.

The shadows grew long as she walked, a big black garbage bag slung over her shoulder with a handful of possessions she'd picked up along the way. She'd found scratched sunglasses in a gas station parking lot. An old towel in a garbage bin the next day. She'd washed it in a creek, and now used it as a towel and as a pillow.

The following day, she'd found a plastic water bottle in a dumpster. It was one of those cheap ones from a dollar store, but it was a gold mine to her.

One of her favorite possessions was a metal dog bowl she'd found alongside the highway. It was a little dented, but that didn't matter. She cleaned it up and used it to boil water. Then she'd let it cool before filling the plastic bottle and drinking all the rest at once.

Her most important possession, though, was one she'd almost failed to get. She'd been walking through a tiny town, population maybe 300, when she spotted two things: a policeman walking her direction on the sidewalk, and a couple of pre-teens trying to light a cigarette.

As she'd looked furtively around for a place to hide from the officer, the kids saw him and took off running down an alley. He gave chase. She quickened her step, and when she reached the spot where they'd been, she saw that they'd dropped a pack of cigarettes. And a lighter!

She'd snatched up that lighter like it was a gift from God, and hurried on her way. How long would it last? She had no idea. But for now, that lighter was a blessing! She had no doubt that boiling her drinking water had spared her from some bad bugs, and that lighter made it possible to start the fires necessary to boil the water.

So things were working out. It might not look like she was living a triumphant life, with her blue cotton dress hanging loosely over her emaciated frame. But she was free. She was not sick. And she was on her way home.

What more could she ask?

WILLOW'S DREAMS were filled with weird, fitful scenes of Jacob and Marcus. She spent much of the night waking from one rest-less dream, only to fall asleep and find another. After hours of this, she finally fell into a deep, troubled sleep.

A light like the sun blinded her, and she shielded her eyes. But she sensed a holy presence and slowly lowered her hands to see the lightning-bright angel. He appeared to be at least ten feet tall. A flaming sword hung at his waist, but didn't burn his snow white robe.

"Should we run?" she asked. "From the fires? From Jacob and Marcus?"

"Not yet." The angel's hair looked like pure gold. His eyes were the brightest blue Willow had ever seen.

"Trouble is coming. You must prepare, and offer help to your neighbors."

"You mean the Andersons?"

He nodded solemnly. "Do not be afraid, daughter of God. Keep your spiritual armor on. You must be tested, and you must be true."

"What does that mean?"

"You will know soon enough. Sufficient unto the day, is the evil thereof."

"Is Jacob coming for us? With Marcus?"

"I cannot say."

"Can't, or won't?" Although she trembled at the sight of the magnificent creature, Willow had to know more. She needed specifics. Details.

"It matters not."

"How will I know what to do?"

"The Spirit will guide you. As He always has." With that, the angel floated into the sky, then zoomed away like a rocket. Willow gasped and awoke.

JACOB'S EYES opened and blinked. His head rested comfortably on a pillow, his back felt relaxed on a decent mattress. He glanced around the room.

A real house. A real bedroom. Raven's bedroom, as it turned out. And a fine room it was, too.

He'd spent a little time straightening the place out when he'd arrived yesterday. Looters had done an impressive job on it, taking most anything of value. Plus, Raven herself had returned at least once since she'd run with her friends to the forest, and collected more of her belongings.

Some of her stuff was still here, though. Including her dirty clothes in the hamper.

Would she return again?

He swung his legs out of bed. It was hard to say. Each return to town was more dangerous for her and the group. He doubted they'd be back. Marcus, on the other hand, was sure they would.

Jacob dressed and went to the kitchen. There was no food. Not even salt. They'd done a good job of cleaning this place out.

Pounding on the front door announced Marcus's arrival.

Jacob opened the door, and Marcus shoved a small brown bag and an insulated drink container into Jacob's hands.

"Hot tea and some food to keep you running. I'm off to work."

Jacob opened the bag and saw a pint jar. It felt warm. "Oatmeal with real cream? How did you get this?"

"I'm still working, aren't I?"

"They pay you in food?"

"You got it, buddy!" Marcus slapped Jacob's shoulder. "Come by the station later. I got some work for you to do."

"Did the city stash food before this all went down? How did they know?"

"Nah, 'course not!" Marcus slid his sunglasses over his eyes. "After the EMP, we commandeered the food at the grocery store. For safe keeping and equitable distribution, and all that. We did distribute the perishables equitably that first week, or it would have spoiled. The rest, non-perishables, we locked up. That's how I'm feeding you, buddy. Work for grub!"

"Huh." Jacob nodded. "But there's real cream – "

"Well, sure! We have some local farmers. It's funny – for decades, the small time farmers were the poorest of the poor. Now they're rich!" Marcus laughed. "They do have to share the wealth, though. With us."

"You mean with the police force?"

"Yeah, man! Desperate people want to steal their milk cows or chickens or whatever, right? So they hire farm guards – us – to keep everything safe. And they pay in whatever they produce. Milk, eggs, yogurt, butter. One place is even making cheese."

"Nice."

"Absolutely. It's easy work. For now. Eventually, it might get too dangerous, if hungry folks form armed mobs. But so far, it's all good. I could hook you up."

"I'll think about it."

"Don't think too long, buddy. I'm not gonna feed you forever." Marcus turned to go. "Don't forget to come by the station this morning."

"Hold on – I need directions to the cemetery."

"For your uncle's grave?"

Jacob nodded.

Marcus removed his sunglasses.

"That was a sad business. Real sad." He frowned, then turned and pointed up the street. "Take this road straight west until you see Highline Drive. Go left there, up the long hill, and you'll see a sign for Pinecrest Road on the right. Follow that for about a quarter mile, and you'll be there."

"Where's his grave?"

"Northwest corner. Second row, just a few spaces in. Nice headstone. You can't miss it."

"Okay." Jacob looked again in the paper bag. "Thanks for breakfast."

"You got it. See you in a couple hours."

WILLOW DECIDED NOT to mention the angel. Not yet. She dished up the rice and eggs mixture that Raven had concocted for breakfast, careful to put just enough on each person's plate so everybody would get some. But not much.

They all sat on the grass in front of the cabin to eat after Clark blessed the food.

She took a bite, slowly chewing the carb and protein blend, and studied the smoke plume on the mountain to the south. It seemed to be a little smaller this morning than it had been last night.

That would make sense, though, because the nights at this elevation were quite chilly. The fire would grow more during the heat of the day. Rain could slow it down or even put it out if it wasn't too big yet.

Willow studied the sky. Hazy blue. Not a single cloud.

She sighed.

"What're you thinking?" Raven watched her expression.

Willow pointed south.

"Just looking at the smoke. Wishing for rain."

"That's not likely." Raven set down her fork. "And if we get some this month, it'll probably come in a thunderstorm. Lots of lightning, to start more fires."

Willow ate her last bite.

"Yeah." She stood up. "I need to check in on the Andersons. See if we can help them, and check out that fire. Do you want to come?"

"You bet!" Raven's glossy black hair swept her toned arms as she rose to her feet. "How soon do we leave?"

Uncle Tony came over toward them. His face looked pale. "You're going somewhere?"

"We're going to see if we can help the Andersons." Raven eyed her uncle. "Are you feeling okay?"

"I'm tired."

"Why don't you stay here today and rest?"

He nodded slowly. "Maybe I'll teach the newcomers some foraging skills. It's too late for strawberries, but huckleberries are coming on, and Oregon grapes."

"There's always dandelion greens." Willow pointed to the clearing. "They grow like weeds."

"That's because they *are* weeds," Raven laughed. "Not bad for salads, though."

"Maybe we should try them in a stir fry," Willow said. "With our mushrooms."

"Be careful with the mushrooms." Tony set his hat on his head. "Many are poisonous."

"I think a foraging lesson is a great idea." Willow smiled at him. "Maybe take Matt and Josh, too, after they finish their chores. They know a lot, but we all could learn more from you."

As Tony gathered the group for his impromptu class, Raven and Willow filled their water bottles and donned their nearly-empty backpacks. Then Willow pulled Clark aside.

"Please keep your eyes open. In case Jacob shows up with Marcus or whatever."

"I will do that." His dark eyes were as solemn as his voice. "And Alan will, too."

"Thanks. We'll be back as soon as we can."

The morning grew hot as Willow and Raven made their way to John and Jeannie's retreat. They stopped at a creek to filter water into their depleted bottles. Willow plunged her hands into the clear, cold water, and splashed some on her face. It provided a shocking relief to the heat in her cheeks.

Raven eyed her with concern.

"You're red as a tomato!"

"You would be, too, if you weren't blessed with brown skin."

Raven's eyebrows lifted. "Blessed? Not too many would agree with that."

"Well, you won't burn and peel. Or blister."

"That is true, my friend. We rarely peel or blister."

They continued on, and the air grew smokier as they walked, until a grey haze filled the air. Eventually, they reached the ridge at the rear of the retreat.

"Let's go slow, now, and stay in the open," Willow said. "They usually have guards posted, and I want them to see who we are."

"They still have guards? There's only four of them left!"

"I guess they want to keep all four."

They crested the ridge and started down the hill. As the forest thinned, Willow made out the back of the house, then the barn. She didn't see anyone outside.

She did see smoke, though, and plenty of it. It irritated her eyes and turned the sun orange-red.

Raven sneezed. "Ugh, this is bad."

"I'd say the fire is kicking up."

"Yeah, no kidding."

A moment later, a great rumbling noise filled the forest. Then the ground bucked, sending both Willow and Raven momentarily into the air.

Willow landed on her rear, with a jarring protest from her tailbone. The rumble continued, but was outdone by a great cracking noise.

She looked up and saw the top half of a huge fir snap off and begin to fall toward Raven, who was still sprawled on the ground where she'd landed.

"Look out!" Willow screamed.

5

J acob pulled a weed from beside his uncle's headstone. In the distance, he heard a train rumbling down the tracks. It grew nearer and louder, and suddenly he realized he hadn't heard any trains since the EMP. He looked up just as the ground swelled beneath him. He was thrown into the air like a soccer ball, then dropped with a shudder.

The ground roared as the pulse raced across the cemetery like a wave under the overgrown lawn, lifting and lowering row after row of headstones. Some teetered and toppled, while some landed upright just as they'd been for sixty years or more.

From his vantage point, he watched as the earthquake hit Ponderosa, racing through town like a streak of lightning, lifting streets and buckling the blacktop. Downtown, with its two-story brick storefronts dating back over a hundred years, was hit hard.

Jacob stared, horrified, as shop after shop crumbled into loose brick and fell to the sidewalk and street below. Power poles snapped like twigs and fell over, their lines entangling trees, cars, fences, and homes.

A few of those lines carried electricity from the city's hydroelectric dam upriver, and sparks shot from downed lines and transformers, igniting fires in the tall, dry weeds.

His mouth went dry as he saw homes shake, roofs collapse and walls topple. He looked for Raven's house and saw that it was still standing, along with most of its neighboring homes. People ran out of houses, looking like ants from this distance. He couldn't see anyone running out of the businesses.

Most of them were closed, of course. But if any had been open, their proprietors would need help. If they'd survived the collapsing brick walls.

He rose to his feet, ready to help if he could. But he was knocked over by the first aftershock.

LAURA ARCHER HAD JUST SETTLED into an old barn for a long nap. She tried to do most of her walking very early in the morning and in the evening, because it was cooler then, and she was less likely to be seen. During the long, hot days, she slept. Or at least rested.

She heard the rumble and ran for the door just as the building began to shake, its timbers creaking and moaning in protest. She sprinted outside, the ground shifting and tossing her as she cleared the building.

Sprawling, she tried to find her footing as the ground bounced. The barn behind her groaned. She scrambled and clawed her way into the pasture, away from the sighing, bulging walls. The ground bucked again, then she found her feet and sprinted into the open.

Turning, she watched as the nearest wall collapsed, its hundred-year-old timbers crashing to the floor where she'd slept moments ago. And where she'd left her very few, very treasured, possessions.

TONY POKED his walking pole at a green plant.

"Anybody recognize this?" He glanced at the blank faces gathered around him in the meadow. Deborah crouched down to examine the plant.

"It looks like old asparagus."

"Bingo! Two points for Deborah, zero points for everybody else." He winced a little as a pain squeezed his heart. "And like the asparagus you should have been growing at home, it ripens in the spring. This time of year, it's no good."

A rumble filled the air.

"Everybody sit down!" Alan boomed. "Now!"

Fear twisted the pretty features of Alan's granddaughters as they obeyed, along with the rest of the group. A moment later, the ground swelled and kicked, and they would have been knocked off their feet.

Around the perimeter of the meadow, trees crashed into and over one another, filling the forest with the loudest cacophony Tony had ever heard. Well, outside of some especially loud concerts, maybe.

The pain around his heart tightened like a noose.

IN SLOW MOTION, Willow watched Raven scramble toward her as the tree top crashed down through a neighboring tree's branches. Raven stretched a hand out, and Willow yanked her away from the kill zone. The tree top hit the ground so hard it bounced and broke into three long logs.

Raven screamed as the skinniest piece fell on them.

Willow rolled out of the branches and lurched to her feet. A large branch pinned Raven's left leg to the ground, while other branches poked around her face and neck. Willow grabbed branches of the big fir with both hands, and pulled as hard as she could. The tree top barely budged.

"Can you wiggle out?" She yelled.

"I'm trying!"

"Are you bleeding?"

"I don't know!" Raven's muffled response filled Willow with more urgency, and she pulled with super-human strength.

"I'm almost out! Keep pulling!"

Willow dug in with her feet and threw all her weight against the tree. Which wasn't a lot, since she'd been eating so little this summer.

"I'm out!" Raven crawled out of the branches. Her jeans were torn. Blood seeped into the denim along a rip at her thigh.

"You're bleeding." Willow scrambled toward her. "Let me look."

The ground rumbled again, and the forest shook with its fury as an aftershock hit. Willow flung her arms around her friend as the ground sank and bucked.

Nausea swirled her stomach and threatened to rise in her throat. But breakfast had been small, and enough time had passed that her stomach was empty. Nothing came up.

The ground rested. Motion ceased. The forest fell silent.

Willow let go of Raven.

"I need to look at your leg."

"Right." Raven pulled at the rip in her pants. "It's just a big scratch."

"We'll need to get it cleaned, though. It's long, and it's full of tree bark junk." She checked out her friend's eyes. "Are you okay otherwise?"

"I think so." Raven stretched out her arms and legs. "A little sore."

"We can live with that."

Willow turned her attention to the Andersons' house. The masonry enclosing the chimney had pulled away from the exterior wall and now lay broken on the ground. But the walls still stood, and the roof appeared sound. It was impressive.

She glanced toward the barn. It had survived, as well. Then she noticed a tree had fallen on the rear portion of the roof. And the door from one of the horse's stalls to the paddock was shaking violently. It looked like a horse was kicking it to get out.

"Where is everybody?" Raven asked.

"I have no idea." Willow brushed bits of tree bark from her clothing. "Let's get the animals out of the barn, and then we'll go find the Andersons."

As they hurried toward the barn, Willow's thoughts turned toward home. Was her brother okay? Her friends? Hopefully they'd been in a safe place when the earthquake hit.

Raven beat her to the barn, and flung open the man door.

"You wait here," Willow said. "Stay back from the walls."

Willow ran inside, opened the gates to let the cows and horses out, and raced back outside. Both Brown Swiss cows trotted out then stopped and looked around, while the horses rushed out and galloped, wild-eyed, around and around their paddock. They bucked and kicked and snorted.

"Must have been scary in there," Raven said.

"It was scary out here, too." Willow looked toward the house. "Let's go see where everyone went."

They let themselves in the unlocked back door, hurried through the kitchen and living room.

"Anybody home?" Raven called out.

No one answered.

"Let's check downstairs," Willow said. "I don't know where they could be!"

They checked the daylight basement, but no one was there.

"Do you think they bugged out already?" Willow asked. "They were thinking about leaving because of the fire."

"Maybe." Raven pursed her lips, then shook her head. "No. They would have taken the animals if they'd evacuated. Maybe not all the chickens, but at least the cows and horses."

"That's true." They walked outside, and Willow's gaze turned to the south. The smoke billowed above the hilltop. "Since we can't find them, let's go check out the fire. We should find out how big it is."

"Okay, but let's make it quick. We need to get back and check on our cabin and our friends." Raven led the way in an easy jog down the driveway, across the forest service road, over a small hill and down a steep incline to a creek. They splashed water on their faces, then hiked up the long, heavily wooded hill to the crest of the mountain.

Smoke filled the air, dropping grey-white ash in their hair. Willow looked at Raven and burst out laughing.

"You look like an old Indian lady with grey hair!"

Raven narrowed her eyes. "Hey, white chick, don't you be calling me old!"

They laughed, then coughed.

"It's not real good to breathe this stuff," Raven said. "Let's take a look, and get out of here."

They found some boulders that provided a decent vantage point, and scrambled up near the top.

"Whoa!" Raven's eyes grew large. "Take a look at that!"

Willow climbed up on Raven's boulder and looked down the hill toward the fire.

"Holy smokes!" Willow whispered.

Far below, the fire turned trees into flaming torches. It threw burning pine cones, like firebombs, into the dry weeds and grass, which quickly ignited new fires beyond the periphery of the main blaze.

A breeze fanned the flames, pushing it up the hill toward them. Intermittent snaps and cracks sounded as the fire consumed the forest, but the primary noise was a roar, like a huge furnace.

Her face grew hot, and Willow imagined it was from the fire more than the sunny July day.

"Let's get out of here!" Raven stepped down to a lower boulder.

But Willow didn't move. She stared at the flaming forest, breathing the smoke and feeling the ash settling on her head. The flames, the sounds, the doom – it was mesmerizing. She couldn't turn away.

Raven grabbed her hand.

"Willow!" She pulled. "Let's go!"

She gagged, then coughed, then let Raven lead her off the boulders.

"Wait! I think I saw something!" She pulled her hand free and climbed back up the boulders. "It's blue."

Willow stared along the ridge of the mountain, willing her eyes to see through the heavy grey smoke. Then she saw it again. Somebody wearing a blue t-shirt!

"I see somebody!" She pointed east along the ridge. "It's probably the Andersons!"

She leapt down from the rocks.

"Are you sure?" Raven asked. "Let's be careful, in case it's not them."

"Right. But I'm pretty sure it is them."

They moved quietly but quickly east, until they could make out the person in the blue t-shirt. It was Jeannie Anderson. Not far beyond her was John, with their friends Mike and Julie. They were walking north, toward their home.

"Hey!" Willow jumped up and down, waving. "Over here!"

Jeannie turned their way, startled. John's hand moved toward his holster.

"It's me, Willow!" She waved again, and started toward them. "And Raven!"

The Andersons closed the distance. Jeannie gave them big hugs.

"What are you two doing out here?" John asked.

"We came to see you," Willow said. "And to see the fire."

"How about those earthquakes?" Jeannie asked. "Worst I've ever felt."

"We were checking on the fire when the earthquakes hit," John said. "But now I'm more worried about whether our house survived the quakes."

"It did," Willow said. "Except the chimney."

"Oh, thank God!" Jeannie exclaimed. "How about the barn?"

"It's standing, but a tree fell on the back part. It'll need some repairs." Willow brushed ash off her shoulder. "The animals were freaked, though, so we let them out."

They started down the hill together.

"What are you going to do?" Willow glanced at John as they walked. "I mean, are you evacuating?"

"I think we'll have to." He shot a sad look at his wife. "Hopefully, the fire won't hit our place, but that wildfire is too big to take the risk of staying."

"Where will you go?" Raven asked.

"You're welcome to stay with us," Willow said. "But we might leave, too. Not just because of the fire, but because of Jacob."

John frowned. "I still can't make sense of that. You think he's collaborating with the police to turn in people who didn't get the mark?"

"He is!" Raven said. "He's with my brother, Marcus, who is one of the guys in charge of making sure everyone gets chipped."

"Huh." John removed his hat and brushed the ash off it. "Jacob seemed like he was one of us."

"If he's a spy, that's his job!" Raven's voice rose. "To be convincing. Then to find out who we all are, and where to find us!"

"So, what does this guy Marcus look like?" John asked. "I'll take him out if I see him."

"John!" Jeannie exclaimed.

"What? This is a war, Jeannie." He looked back at Raven. "I guess he's Native?"

"No. He's white."

John's eyebrows rose a little as a genuinely confused look crossed his face. "I thought he's your brother."

"Half-brother, actually. Our dad is white. My mom was Kootenai. His mom is white." She paused. "It's even more confusing because Marcus's last name is the same as our dad, but I was given my tribal name of Deepwater."

She frowned slightly. "Anyway, I don't want him killed. Stopped, yes. But not murdered."

"Of course not!" Jeannie said.

"Hopefully it won't come to that." John stepped across a log and reached back to give his wife a hand.

At the creek, Raven and Willow stopped to wash the ash out of their hair, while the Andersons and their friends hurried back to their home. The cold water dripping down Willow's back brought wonderful relief from the heat.

"I really want to get home quick and check on everyone, but I feel like we need to help the Andersons if we can," she told Raven as they neared the house.

"Sounds good to me. I want to check on Uncle Tony, especially," Raven said. "He hasn't been feeling well. I'm glad he decided to spend a little time with us."

"Yeah. He has so much knowledge. We need to soak it all up

like sponges." Willow tapped on the door before entering the house. "Knock, knock!"

"We're in the living room," Jeannie called. "C'mon in."

Mike, Julie and the Andersons each had a backpack on the floor, and they were dividing things to put in them.

Willow's stomach soured. The scene reminded her of bugging out from her own home in Ponderosa with Josh, Matt and Raven. Was that only a few weeks ago? It seemed like another lifetime.

She frowned when she thought of the things the Andersons would have to leave behind. Family photos. Beloved heirlooms. Furniture. Jewelry. More importantly, the incredible stash of food and supplies they'd carefully stored up for years, along with the retreat itself and all it included – clean running water, appliances that still worked, comfortable beds, and all the best meanings of the word, *home*.

"What can we do to help?" she asked.

John looked up. "You can take some of the chickens. We can't take them all with us, and we'll need a new starter flock after the fire, if we lose the rest."

"You should take the adolescent ones," Jeannie said. "We can catch them and put them in a couple cardboard boxes. You sure you don't mind?"

"Not at all," Willow assured her. "I wish we could do more."

"You can." Jeannie's eyes glistened. "I want you to take some of my jewelry and a few of our photos. We'll take some, too, but...."

"I understand. We brought almost empty packs, so feel free to load us up. And please, let us help in any way we can. That's why we came."

John's face was long as he studied the girls. "We'll load you up with food. You all can use it, and who knows if any will still be here a week from now if we leave it."

"That's incredibly generous," Raven said. "But we didn't come here for that."

"I know." John looked at the pile of possessions on the floor. "But we should have offered more sooner. What a waste, if it all goes up in flames."

"We'll pray that won't happen." Willow looked at John, then Jeannie. "We'll pray the fire will miss your place."

"And yours." Jeannie got to her feet. "C'mon, let's get you girls loaded up so you can get out of here. I'm sure you want to get back and check on your own group."

"You never mentioned where you're going," Raven said. "Do you have a plan?"

"We aren't exactly sure yet," John said. "You girls have lived here your whole lives. Do you have any ideas?"

Willow furrowed her brow. "Normally, I'd say, camp out anywhere, but the forest is full of people trying to survive off the fish and deer. I imagine the campgrounds are packed, too, for the same reason. But you could try that, I guess. The trick will be protecting your livestock. People will definitely steal whatever they can, because they're starving."

"I have a weird idea," Raven volunteered. "This sounds counterintuitive, so it might just work."

An intrigued look crossed Jeannie's face. "What is it?"

"You could go stay at my house in town for a while. It should be vacant. Although you'll have to be careful, because that's where Uncle Tony saw Marcus and Jacob. They were probably just looking for me, so I doubt they'll be back."

"That's crazy!" Willow stared at her friend. "It's on the edge of town! All those people...."

"It is crazy, and that's why it might work," John said. "We could just blend in. And if anyone asks, we could say we're passing through and we used to be friends of the owner."

Raven smiled. "You *are* friends of the owner."

"I still think it's nuts," Willow said. "But if you're considering it, you should consider my place. It's just down the road from hers, and we have a small barn where you could keep your livestock and chickens out of sight."

John took a small notebook and pen from his front pocket. "Let me get the addresses and some directions from you. I don't know if we'll actually go there. But who knows? We don't have a lot of options."

6

Jacob's breath came in gasps as he reached the edge of town. It had been all downhill, but it was a good distance, and he'd sprinted.

He stopped and looked around. Downtown was to his left, and a residential neighborhood was to his right. Where should he go first?

Maybe he could pull someone from the rubble of the bricks in the business district, but there were a lot more people in the neighborhood, and it might be easier to get to them, since they were less likely to be crushed under three stories' of rubble.

The nearest house was a ranch-style 1960's brick home. Gaping cracks snaked up the front wall where the masonry had cracked apart. He hurried toward it.

"Anybody home?" He yelled as he jogged up the walk. "You guys okay?"

He stopped at the door and pounded on it. No one responded. He yelled and pounded again, but still got no response. Maybe no one was home.

Three homes down, he saw a boy exit a front door. The kid

couldn't have been older than four. He was holding his knee and shrieking. Where were his parents? Had they been injured?

Jacob hustled over to the kid.

"Are you okay, buddy?"

Tears streaked his dirty face as he shook his head. Other than his bloody knee, he appeared uninjured.

"Is your mommy home?"

The child nodded, his black hair flopping over his forehead as he pointed through the door.

"She fell," he sobbed.

"I'm going to check on her," Jacob said. "You stay here in the front yard, okay?"

The boy gulped and nodded again.

"Okay, I'll be right back, and we'll fix up your knee." Jacob wasn't sure how he'd fix it, with no first aid supplies or even a bandage, but the words seemed to calm the child.

He knocked on the open door before entering.

"Hello! Can anyone hear me?" He stepped into a messy living room strewn with toys and puzzle pieces. The drapes were drawn, and it took his eyes a moment to adjust to the darkness.

"Hello?"

The television had been thrown off its shelf and lay broken on the floor, along with some knickknacks.

Jacob stepped carefully into the kitchen. Cupboard doors were flung open, their contents dumped to the floor and countertops. A white dusting of flour sifted over shattered dishes on the grey tile.

He stepped through the mess and found a hallway.

"Hello? I'm here to help!" He pushed open the first door. It was clearly the child's bedroom, with a small bed and a little dresser. And a super hero poster on the wall.

The next door opened into a bathroom. The earthquake had

tossed open the medicine cabinet, spilling toiletries into the sink.

He continued to the next door. A small office. A tall, heavy wooden bookcase had tipped and fallen, pinning a petite woman with brown skin and black hair. She wasn't moving. At all.

Jacob knelt and touched her shoulder.

"Hey, can you hear me?"

She didn't respond. Was she even breathing?

He pulled her arm free of some books, and felt for a pulse. It was difficult to say if he was feeling her heartbeat, or just an echo of his own.

He had to get the bookcase off her. Had to get her out from under all this, and see if she was still alive.

What if she wasn't?

The little boy appeared in the doorway, a blue blanket under his arm. He ran toward the woman and flung himself at her.

"Momma!"

UNCLE TONY'S hand shot to his chest as the pain tightened around his heart. Was this it? Was he going out with a heart attack during an earthquake aftershock?

He tried to suck in a deep breath, but couldn't get enough air. It was like a python had wrapped around his chest and was squeezing the life out of him.

He looked up, and his eyes met Clark's. The young black man scrambled toward him, worry etched across his forehead.

"Are you alright?"

Another aftershock rattled them, knocking Clark to the ground. He crawled the rest of the distance to reach Tony's side.

"You are in pain?" His accent softened his words.

"Can't breathe," Tony squeezed out, still clutching at his chest. "My heart!"

Until this moment, he'd believed he wasn't afraid of death. But now, standing at the door, he was terrified to let himself go through.

"I will pray!" Clark pulled Tony toward him, his left arm supporting Tony's shoulders, and his right hand clamping down on Tony's chest. He turned his face toward heaven.

"Heavenly Father, I pray you will release Tony from this pain. Jesus, I pray your stripes will heal our friend. That his arteries will open and his heart and lungs will be released from this attack. Holy Spirit, please flow your healing breath through Tony's body. Please Lord, heal him and let him stay with us. I rebuke all the plans of the devil for Tony and his health. In Jesus' name, AMEN!"

As the ground settled from its shaking, Tony took a staggered breath and was able to fill his lungs with sweet oxygen. He gulped another breath.

The python released its coils around his chest. His heart relaxed, the pain easing away as if he'd imagined it.

He looked into Clark's concerned face.

"Whoa." He rubbed his chest to see if it was really okay. He sat up. "If that doesn't beat all."

He looked again at Clark, as if seeing him for the first time.

"Are you an angel?"

White teeth flashed a huge grin across Clark's face.

"You feel better! Praise Jesus!" He raised his arms to the sky. "Thank you, Lord!"

Jaci left her daughters and scrambled toward them.

"What's going on?"

Clark wrapped an arm around her. "You mean, besides the earthquakes?"

Her gaze met Tony's.

"Are you okay?"

Tony nodded.

"I'm more than okay. Your husband, here, has a gift!"

IT WAS mid-afternoon by the time Willow and Raven approached the cabin. Three times, they'd been rattled by significant aftershocks. Twice, they'd dropped their boxes of young chickens. And once, the chickens had escaped one of the dropped cardboard boxes, and the girls had spent half an hour catching them all.

On top of all that, their backpacks were bulging and heavy with food the Andersons had sent home. The July sun beat on their heads as the wildfire filled their lungs with smoke.

By the time the cabin came into view, Willow couldn't imagine a time she'd been happier to get home.

And that old cabin was still standing, not a scratch on it, nor a log out of joint.

She breathed a prayer of thanks.

Raven seemed quieter than normal this afternoon, but that was understandable. It was a long, hot hike. Willow wasn't that talkative herself.

She just wanted to drop off her load, then go soak in the creek. That cold water was a true blessing. This time of year, it provided a swimming hole and a cool bath, in addition to water for all the people and animals to drink.

As they crossed the clearing to the cabin, Raven finally spoke.

"Do you think John will kill Marcus?"

"What? No." Willow stopped and stared at her friend. "I think he was just blowing smoke. Saying what he felt, not what he's actually planning."

"I hope you're right." Raven didn't look convinced. "Because even if Marcus were dead, there's still Jacob. He's the one who knows to find us. He could lead a new group of agents here, just as easily as he could bring Marcus."

"I know."

"Do you think we should move?"

"Not yet." Willow frowned.

"Why not?"

"I had a dream last night."

"A vision? With the angel?"

"Yeah. I asked about leaving, and was told to stay for now."

"Until when?" Raven swatted a fly buzzing her face.

"I'm not sure."

"That's not very helpful."

"It's all we need to know for now. God guides us day by day, hour by hour. We're not supposed to worry about tomorrow. Sufficient unto the day is the evil thereof, right?"

"That's for sure." Raven walked to the cabin door. "And this day has had its fair share already."

She pulled open the door and looked inside.

"Where do you suppose everyone is?"

"Your uncle was taking them foraging, remember? Maybe they're still out learning how to eat weeds." Willow set the box of chickens on the floor and squirmed out of her backpack. "I don't think we'll need to eat too many weeds tonight, with all this good food the Andersons sent over."

Raven grinned as she opened her pack and pulled out two jars of sauce.

"Can you believe it? Spaghetti sauce and real pasta! I'm not eating weeds tonight. We're having a feast!"

～

AFTER THE THIRD AFTERSHOCK, Laura Archer stared at the collapsed barn. Her possessions were all under that rubble. Could she dig them out? Would they all be destroyed, flattened by the falling timbers?

She approached the fallen building. Maybe something could be salvaged. She had to try.

Her water bottle, dog dish and lighter were necessary to her survival, and would be so difficult to replace. Impossible, maybe.

But the barn timbers were massive, and she had no gloves to protect her hands from the splinters. Perhaps she could pry some of the smaller boards away and see if she could reach her things.

Her cotton dress swirled around her knees as she grabbed a board. It was still nailed to a beam on one end. She yanked and pulled. And got nowhere.

"Hey! What're you doing?"

The rough male voice behind her made her jump. She whirled around.

He was about her age, maybe 45, dressed in stained mechanic's overalls, a red t-shirt, and a straw hat. His right hand gripped a shotgun.

"I don't want any trouble." Laura backed up a step.

"Then you might explain what you're doing to our barn." He stepped toward her, and she caught a whiff of his foul breath.

"I'm not causing it any damage, that's for sure. I was just looking for something I dropped."

His eyes narrowed. "You dropped something in our barn?"

She couldn't back up anymore without scrambling onto the rubble. Which was something she actually considered.

"Like I said, I don't want any trouble." With her peripheral vision, she searched for an escape path around him. She'd have to move fast, and hope he didn't shoot her. "I'll just be on my way."

"Not so fast, little lady." His dark eyes looked soulless. "Maybe I can help you find what you're looking for."

She doubted it, but decided to play along until she could get away.

"A water bottle," she said. "And a lighter."

"A cigarette lighter?" He glowered. "What were you gonna do with that? Light our barn up?"

He encroached further into her personal space. And he reeked of pungent body odor.

"What are ya, a little pyro?"

"Of course not." She tried not to gag. "They're for cigarettes."

He eyed her suspiciously. "You got smokes?"

She pointed to the ground about ten feet behind him, to his right. As he turned to look, she made a break for it, leaping past his left shoulder and racing toward the safety of the forest.

7

As her little boy shrieked at his elbow, Jacob tried CPR on the petite woman for nearly twenty minutes. She never regained a pulse. Never took a breath. She was long gone.

Getting the bookcase off her had taken several minutes and massive effort. And who knew how long she'd lain under it before he arrived? A huge gash on her head suggested she'd hit something hard as she fell. Maybe her head had smashed the wooden desk, or maybe all the damage was from the falling bookcase.

In any event, she was gone and she wasn't coming back. And her son seemed to have some understanding of that, even as young as he was.

Jacob picked the kid up. He struggled and kicked, and Jacob held him tighter. Finally, he relaxed into Jacob's shoulder and sobbed. Tears and saliva soaked through Jacob's black t-shirt.

What was he going to do with this little guy? Where was his father?

He carried the boy down the hall, through the trashed

kitchen, and out through the dark living room into the bright sunshine. He set him down on the steps and squatted down to his eye level.

"What's your name?"

"Danny." The little boy sniffled.

"My name is Jacob."

The boy's eyes met his.

"Danny, do you know where your daddy is?"

He shook his head, his gaze dropping to the steps. He started crying again.

"Have you seen your daddy today?"

"No." He rubbed grubby hands against his eyes. "We never see him."

Oh, great. He had a dead mom and a deadbeat dad? Now what?

Jacob looked around. Across the street, a woman swept broken glass into a dustpan. Jacob grabbed the kid's hand and walked over to her.

"Excuse me."

She turned to him. Bright blue eyes sparkled behind black-framed glasses. Her blonde hair was neatly done up.

"Yes?"

Jacob swallowed. She was slim and young and really pretty.

"Uh, I was wondering...." He had to stop staring and start talking. "I wondered if you know this boy's dad. He lives across the street."

"Danny lives across the street. But his dad doesn't."

"Right." He tried to look at her eyes and not her dress. It was a short, red summer dress that revealed... a lot. "Um, his mom was killed in the quake. I need to find his dad."

"What?" Her hand shot to her ruby lips. "Oh, no!"

Big blue eyes turned to the child and filled with tears.

"I can't believe it." Those mesmerizing eyes turned back to Jacob. "How?"

TONY SAW his niece as he approached the cabin with his foraging friends.

"How'd it go, Uncle Tony?" Raven shaded her eyes from the afternoon sun as she glanced at the group. "Looks like you all made it through the earthquakes unscathed."

"I didn't get to teach as much as I hoped, but we made progress." His blue eyes twinkled. "How about you?"

"We brought back food from the Andersons. They're getting ready to evacuate." She paused, studying him. "You look better this afternoon."

"Clark prayed for me." He smiled.

"Good!" Then her countenance turned somber. "That wildfire is getting out of control. We may have to pack up ourselves."

"It would be good to make some plans, just in case." He watched Willow step out of the cabin. She approached them.

"Raven and I were talking about plans for evacuating. Because of the fire," he told her.

"We're going to stay put for now." Willow glanced at Raven. "But maybe not for long. I think we should haul a lot of water from the creek. Fill up all the containers we can find."

Tony shook his head. "You can't fight a wildfire with a few buckets and bottles. You'll be barbequed."

"No, of course not." She pointed toward the cabin and barn. "But if we have time, maybe we can soak those shake roofs."

He gazed at the pioneer buildings. Except for a few repairs over the decades, those cedar shakes had to be eighty to a hundred years old. Dry as parchment in the desert. He drew and released a long breath, then shrugged.

"Can't hurt, I guess. If you have time."

"After dinner, I'm going to ask everyone to help soak the garden. The more water we can get on it, the better," Willow said. "Especially if we do have to leave."

"If you have to leave, the garden will die," Tony said. "Unless you expect to return in a day or two. It'll wither up quick in this heat."

A slight frown turned her lips. "Well, we have to try. And maybe we won't have to evacuate, right?"

"Let's hope not." Tony didn't mention his other reasons for hoping the group didn't have to evacuate. Clark's prayers had done wonders today, but what would happen next time his heart acted up? This sure hadn't been the first time.

LAURA RACED toward the forest as the creepy man yelled and cursed behind her. She didn't look back, but pumped her arms as she sprinted for the concealment of the nearest trees. Hopefully his yelling meant he wasn't running.

And hopefully he wasn't aiming that shotgun at her.

Just a few more seconds, and she'd reach the woods. The toe of her left shoe caught in a pocket gopher hole, and she tripped, sprawling forward. She thrust her hands out to break her fall.

Her face was spared as her hands and wrists took the assault. She glanced over her shoulder as she scrambled to her feet.

He was coming! And fast!

Who would've imagined that overweight, middle-aged guy could move so quickly?

Her shoe had come off in the gopher hole, but she didn't have time to retrieve it. She launched herself forward like a rocket into the wilderness. If she could just get into those trees, she could hide, or climb, or something!

AFTER JACOB EXPLAINED how he'd found Danny and his mother, the pretty blonde neighbor introduced herself as Heidi.

"Why don't you two come in, and we'll fix up that skinned knee, have some lemonade and figure out what to do?" Heidi smiled sadly at the boy.

"Lemonade? Really?" Jacob couldn't imagine how Heidi could have such a thing now, so long after the EMP and grocery store closure. It wasn't like lemons grew in Montana! And you couldn't run to the store to get some.

"It's powdered!" She giggled. "I've been saving it for a special occasion."

She thought *this* was a special occasion? A devastating earthquake that killed her neighbor?

But Danny took the hand she offered, and followed her through her door. So Jacob followed her, too.

"I was cleaning up the broken glass first." Heidi stepped over some books and framed photos before walking into the kitchen. "I was going to straighten up the rest of it afterwards."

She pulled three mismatched glasses from the back of the cabinet.

"Most of them broke," she explained. "But four survived. I lost nearly all my plates and bowls, too. Guess I'm going to become a minimalist, whether I want to or not!"

As Heidi poured water from a plastic jug into the glasses and stirred the lemonade mix into them, Jacob's thoughts roamed to the mountains and the fugitives there. Raven, Willow and their crew would be thrilled to have all the dishes and kitchen gear that Heidi considered minimalist.

Those girls were the opposite of Heidi, with her manicured nails and perfect lipstick. They were natural. The jeans and t-shirt type. Or at least they seemed to be.

But who knew? He'd only known them out in the wilderness. Maybe before all that, they were carefully groomed and dainty. It was hard to imagine, though.

It was almost like they were born to the forest. Sure, they were skinny and they struggled, but they were naturally tough and resilient. They were attractive that way.

Heidi handed the smallest glass to Danny and the largest one to Jacob. She was attractive in totally different ways. Here, in the middle of the country's collapse, maybe in the end of the world, she still took care of herself.

Dressed up, fixed her hair, and offered lemonade to a stranger.

"Thanks." He took a sip. It was a bit weak, but it was refreshing.

"Sorry it's not cold. I had the jug out on the porch overnight, but it's warmed up already."

"It's fine." He watched her move around the kitchen, putting things away. Something about her graceful yet flighty movements reminded him of a butterfly. Then she got a cloth to clean Danny's bloodied knee. She held it under the faucet and turned on the tap. Nothing happened.

"Darn it!" Her perfect lips pouted. "Looks like we're out of water. Again."

"The earthquake probably mangled the water lines," Jacob said.

"I hope they'll get them fixed soon. Last time, it was weeks! Or seemed like it, anyway."

Jacob didn't respond. He didn't expect Ponderosa's broken water lines to be fixed anytime in the near future. Not this year, at least. Where would they get any new lines? How would they ship them here? How could they even place an order for them?

Nah, Ponderosa was out of water, like everywhere else in the country probably was, if the EMP was that extensive. Lucky for this town, though, they had the river and the creeks.

They could use buckets to haul it to their homes. Like Willow hauled water for her cabin and garden. The Andersons, they had a sweet place with gravity-fed water. Unless their lines broke, too. Then they'd be in the same boat as everyone else. But he bet they had some plumbing components stored away somewhere for an occasion like this. They were preppers, after all.

"So, do you know where I can find Danny's dad?" Jacob asked.

LAURA MADE it to the trees and began zig-zagging through them. Pain sliced through her bare foot, but she kept going. She didn't glance back to see if the creepy man was still on her tail.

She didn't know what his deal was, but he stank of pure evil.

It was as if the EMP collapse brought out all the worst in people. The ones who might have been marginally criminal before now gave full rein to their impulses, cheating, stealing, shooting and worse. What was to stop them? Not the cops, that was for sure.

In most of the little towns she'd hiked through, there was no evidence of law enforcement anywhere. They must have retreated home to take care of their own families.

Her breath turned to gasps as she ran out of energy. She'd basically been on a starvation diet for weeks. She was in no shape to be running sprints, much less marathons.

Finally, she glanced back. Mr. Creepy Evil was falling behind. If she could keep going, he'd eventually lose interest and go home. Hopefully.

She put on a burst of speed. Maybe the last one she had

enough energy for. At this point, she just needed him to feel discouraged and quit.

Please, God, make him stop!

Pressing on, she dodged more trees until it felt like her lungs would burst. She was too tired, too worn out for this. Her foot blazed and throbbed. No doubt she'd sliced it open on the quack grass and rocks. She was lucky she hadn't perforated it with a stick on the ground.

The further she ran, the more garbage it was picking up. A great way to start an impressive infection.

She needed her feet to be sound and healthy. How else would she be able to complete her journey home?

WHEN THE AIR cooled that evening, Willow organized a bucket brigade to haul water from the creek.

"First, we'll soak the garden really good. We'll make sure the chickens have all they can drink, and we'll take the goats and Gilligan to the creek again. Then we'll fill every container we can find. We'll filter water into all our bottles, and we'll start soaking the roofs."

She turned to the new family. "You guys might want to remove any flammable material from around your cabin site. Brush, dry grass, anything like that."

Clark nodded. "We will help you with the garden and animals first. Then we will work at our cabin until dark."

Uncle Tony spoke up.

"These are good ideas, but don't think they'll save your homes from a wildfire. In a big fire, none of this will matter."

"We know that." Willow twirled a lock of auburn hair around her finger. "But we have to take every precaution. None of us know whether the fire will come this direction. If a few embers fly this way, it'd be good if they didn't burn down the cabin, right?"

Even as she spoke, she could smell smoke. She glanced south and watched the angry grey plume reach toward the sky. That thing was growing. What if it did come their way?

8

L aura hid in the forest until dark. The creepy guy had given up and left hours ago. But what if he came back to find her? If he had a trained dog, it wouldn't be that difficult. She'd left her scent all over the place. Her foot was bleeding. Truth was, he didn't need a dog to find her. Just a decent flashlight.

She had to take care of her foot, and she had to go back for her shoe.

What if he'd found it and taken it?

How would she ever walk clear to Ponderosa?

Could she make it barefoot?

Not likely.

She sighed, breathed a prayer heavenward, and started back the way she came. At least, she hoped she was going that direction. It was too dark to be certain.

Finding a stout stick about the right height, she used it as half walking stick, half crutch. Tenderly, she limped through the woods, slowly feeling her way forward. And finally, the moon illuminated the field with the collapsed barn. Now, to find that shoe!

She wasn't sure exactly where she'd entered the forest, so she began searching in the pale moonlight. She began right at the edge of the woods, skirting it slowly, then moving in a new arc closer to the barn.

About an hour later, she was convinced that evil man had taken her shoe. Tears came then, exhausted tears and angry ones and finally outright devastated tears.

How would she ever get home?

She cried herself out with one final plea.

Lord. I need my shoe!

A cool breeze calmed her damp face as she wiped away her tears with the backs of her hands.

Then she stood up. No sense staying around here. The creepy guy might return, since he claimed it was his barn. Not that there were any houses nearby. This was a truly old barn, and the original farm house was long lost to time and Montana's turbulent weather.

She turned around and started toward the narrow highway north. Maybe she couldn't make it home. But she would try. What else could she do?

She hadn't gone ten paces when her bare foot caught something flat and soft, and she tripped. Her walking stick saved her from a fall. Her heart leapt.

That had felt like something leather!

Like her lost shoe!

Her hands searched the tall grass until she found it. Hard on one side, soft on the other, and yes! It was her missing shoe.

She clutched it to her. Oh! Thank you, Jesus!

JACOB TUCKED Danny into Raven's bed. The kid was so tired, he was asleep moments after his head hit the pillow. In the morning, he'd find Marcus and ask him what to do about the child.

He'd felt disappointed, but tried to act understanding, when Heidi told him that she couldn't take Danny in for a while. She'd said his dad had been gone for several years, and rumor was, he was in a criminal gang.

She'd also said she didn't have enough to feed herself, and without a man to help provide, by hunting or fishing or working for the farmers, she didn't know if she'd make it. How could she possibly care for an orphan alone?

The way she'd said it made Jacob feel like she was hinting that he should be the man in her life. He didn't even know her!

Sure, desperate times called for desperate measures, but Jacob wasn't desperate. Not yet.

He would like to get married someday. Maybe soon, actually, as life was precarious and dangerous. He'd love to have that connection, that intimacy. But he was hoping for a soul mate, in addition to a pretty face.

Heidi certainly had the pretty face. And figure. Which she'd practically offered to him.

Was she just desperate for a man's provision and protection? Or was she actually attracted to him?

It didn't matter. He wasn't going to get sucked into that trap. Like his namesake, Jacob intended to marry for love.

His stomach growled as he walked downstairs, through the living room, and out to the porch.

The acrid smell of smoke hit him, and it was the gagging smell of house fires, not the simple smoke smell of forest fires. He easily knew the difference from his time as a volunteer firefighter. He turned off his flashlight.

In the distance, he could make out three fires in town. One was fairly small, in the general vicinity of Marcus's house. Maybe it was a burning outbuilding, or maybe a small house, or perhaps a fire that had been controlled by a neighborhood bucket brigade. A little town like Ponderosa could be counted on to form bucket brigades wherever possible. As much to save their own homes as to help their neighbors.

The other two fires were bigger. One appeared to be downtown, in the business district. But the largest one was in a neighborhood at the opposite end of town, not too far from the cemetery where he'd visited his uncle's grave this morning.

That was an area of nice homes. Built on the sloping side of the mountain, the neighborhood overlooked town, with great views of the Bethel River. He imagined the mayor lived there, and the local banker and doctor, and anyone else with enough money for a nice view lot.

Unfortunately for them, their lots were large and populated by beautiful old trees. Also, the hillside that gave them the great views also made them vulnerable to wildfires moving quickly upslope. And when the evening breeze picked up from the river, that wildfire would sweep the whole neighborhood.

He doubted a single home there would be untouched come morning.

But there was nothing he could do. He was stuck here with an orphan kid.

And even if he wasn't, it would take a hundred bucket brigadiers, at least, to attempt to save a single home up there. In the path of an extremely dangerous fire. If a hundred or more volunteers could be found, who weren't trying to solve their own problems from the earthquakes, how would they decide which of the fancy homes to try to save? They couldn't save them all.

Would they flip a coin? Draw straws? Play favorites? It was ridiculous.

And tomorrow, there would be a whole neighborhood of homeless families. Where would they go?

Most likely to the now-vacant homes of the Christians who'd

been captured or killed or who had fled to the mountains. Christians like those who'd lived in the house he was staying in – Christians like Raven and Willow.

Jacob's gaze drifted southeast, toward Willow's wilderness. He didn't know the name of the national forest, but in his mind, that is what it would be. Willow's Wilderness.

Well, at least she wasn't here, stuck in town with fires raging out of control. She was probably peacefully sleeping in her snug little cabin with her friends safe and near. He envied her that.

WILLOW WIPED her brow and set down her bucket. It was dark. Enough for one day. They were all exhausted.

"Let's get some rest. Tomorrow will be here before we know it."

To the south, the eerie glow of the wildfire outlined the ridge behind the Andersons' retreat. Was the fire already to John and Jeannie's property? Had they gone to town, or made another decision about evacuating?

Her back ached. She stretched, then followed Raven into the cabin, climbed into her bunk, and collapsed.

Next thing she knew, it was daylight. Maybe around 5 a.m. She got up and went straight to the door, walked out and looked south. In the daylight, the fire itself was not visible this far away, but the plume was getting larger.

It looked like a thunderhead, a column rising into the atmosphere and mushrooming a bit at the top.

If it didn't rain soon, that fire would be huge and devastating.

Was it headed north? Towards her cabin?

Lord, what should we do?

She felt that they should both stay and go. Or actually, that they should continue soaking the garden and the roofs, but also begin packing for evacuation.

Returning inside, she climbed the loft ladder to wake up Josh and Matt.

"Time to get up, guys! We've got lots to do today!"

As Willow started a fire in the stove to cook eggs for breakfast, Raven climbed out of her bunk and woke up Candy.

Willow began scrambling the eggs, and glanced at Raven.

"Why don't you call Uncle Tony for breakfast? I believe he slept under the stars again, out by the barn."

"Okay, I will." Raven headed out the door.

Candy began combing out her blonde curls. "What's the plan today?"

"We're going to keep soaking the buildings, and we're going to prepare and pack for evacuation." Willow stirred the eggs. "I hope we won't have to leave, but we better be ready if we do. That fire is really something."

"I want to evacuate," Candy said. "Even if there wasn't a fire, I'd want to get out of here because of Marcus and Jacob. I don't want to be here with Maria when they show up."

"Neither do I," Willow admitted. "That's one fight I'd rather not have to face."

"You think we'd lose?" Candy set down her comb and studied Willow with those big blue eyes.

"I don't want to fight Raven's brother. Or Jacob. We thought he was a friend."

"Yeah." Candy frowned. "Until we learned he was friends with our foe."

The door banged open, and Raven walked in.

"Uncle Tony's gone."

"What?" Willow stared at her friend. "He just left? Without saying goodbye?"

"Well, he kinda said goodbye to me last night, but I thought he meant it like 'goodnight.'"

"Huh? That doesn't make any sense." As Willow dished the eggs, the boys came down from the loft. Always on time for a meal, if nothing else. She handed them plates and forks, and shooed them out the door. "Ask a blessing before you dig in."

She turned back to Raven. "What did he say, exactly?"

"It was something like, 'I love you, little bird. See ya later.'"

"Oh." Willow thought about it for a moment. "That sounds like he might have been planning to leave."

"He slept here, though. I saw where the grass was tamped down next to the barn. But all his stuff is gone, so he definitely left." Raven paused. "I just wish he would have said goodbye. So I could say goodbye. Because these days, you never know if you'll see someone you love again. And he said he's been having heart trouble...."

She got a little teary-eyed, and Willow wrapped an arm around her shoulders.

"I know exactly what you mean."

"Of course you do." Raven managed a weak smile. "Your mom. Do you ever wonder...?"

"All the time." Now it was Willow's turn to fight back tears. She bit her lip before plunging ahead. "I wonder if she's alive. If we might ever see her again. On earth, I mean."

She blinked fiercely. Losing her dad was bad enough, especially given the circumstances. She forced herself not to glance toward Candy, who was brushing out little Maria's hair.

"I'm sorry. I have to go outside." She handed Raven the spatula. "Could you finish this?"

Willow fled out the door before Raven had a chance to respond. Matt and Josh looked up, but she just hurried past them, straight toward the creek.

Once there, she splashed cold water on her face, washing off the hot tears. She didn't have time for this. There was work to be done. Decisions to be made. Crises to avert.

If they had to bug out, where would they go? Where do you hide from a wild fire if you live in the forest?

The Andersons might be able to evacuate to Ponderosa, because they didn't really know anybody there, and perhaps they could quietly blend in for a few days. Returning to town was out of the question for Willow's group. They were known in town, and Marcus and Jacob were there – if they weren't, even now, on their way *here*.

She pulled herself together. What if they were approaching? She hurried back toward the cabin.

It was time to get the group packed up. The angel said trouble was coming. He said not to leave "yet." That was yesterday.

Today, she wanted to get ready for the moment she knew, deep in her soul, was near.

JACOB DIDN'T HAVE a scrap of food in the house to feed his little orphan. So as soon as Danny woke up, they set off for Marcus's house. The kid cried for his momma most of the way there, and he walked so slowly that finally Jacob scooped him up and carried him.

Smoke from the fires lay heavy over town, but at least there was no smoke rising from Marcus's neighborhood. That had been the smallest fire he'd seen last night. The downtown fire was still putting out a lot of smoke, but didn't appear to have grown too much.

However, the fire on the western slope, where the nice homes had stood, was steadily advancing uphill into the forest.

Charred skeletons of brick and stone houses stood out among the blackened trunks of now-branchless trees.

Even from this distance, he could see the ground still smoldering in the lower areas that had burned first. Higher up the hill, live flames hungrily consumed dry grass and brush, then licked the trunks of pines and firs and tamaracks. It was going to be an insatiable fire, especially in this dry July heat.

Jacob set Danny down on the sidewalk leading to Marcus's home.

"Okay, here's the deal." He got down to the kid's eye level. "We're going to see my friend Marcus. If you behave yourself, maybe he'll give us something to eat, alright?"

Danny gave one solemn, affirmative nod, his black hair flopping into his brown eyes.

Jacob walked up and knocked on the door. "Marcus?"

"What?" The curt response floated through the screened window.

"It's me, Jacob."

"Hold on!"

He waited. A minute went by, then another. Had Marcus forgotten he was standing on the porch? Or was he just being a jerk?

Finally, the door opened.

Marcus stood in the doorway, wearing a white t-shirt and dirty blue jeans streaked with soot. His hair was tousled like he'd just climbed out of bed. Huge bags underlined bloodshot eyes.

"You okay, man?" Jacob asked.

"I could have used some help last night," Marcus growled. "Where were you?"

Jacob glanced down at Danny. The kid stared at Marcus with huge eyes.

"I was with this little man. Danny."

Marcus stared back at the kid like he'd just noticed him standing there. Perhaps he had. Finally, he spoke.

"Hey, Danny. I'm Marcus." He held out his hand, and the boy shook it.

"I was trying to help folks after the earthquakes, and his mom was killed. I was hoping maybe you could help me find his dad? The neighbor said his name is Brian Higgins."

Marcus guffawed.

"Nah, we won't find him. We've got a mile-long string of warrants out for him. Drunk driving, failure to appear, probation violations, domestic violence, drugs. Mostly misdemeanors, but it would add up to a lot of jail time. He's been gone for years. I don't think he's ever coming back to Montana."

Jacob looked at the kid. Maybe he shouldn't be listening to all this.

"Hey, Danny, why don't you go play in the yard," Jacob said. "Stay where you can see me, though."

The kid hustled off, and Jacob turned back to Marcus.

"What are we gonna do with him?"

"That's your problem, buckwheat!" Marcus grinned. "You should have left him where you found him."

"Alone? Are you kidding?" Jacob couldn't believe his ears. "His mother was dead in the house!"

"One of the neighbors would have taken pity on him."

"Should I take him back, then?"

Marcus snorted. "Hardly! They all noticed you taking him yesterday, trust me. They saw a tender-hearted fool, and they know you can't abandon him now. So they won't volunteer."

"I can't take care of a kid." Jacob frowned and glanced over his shoulder. Danny was playing in the dirt at the corner of Marcus's yard. Truth was, Jacob could hardly take care of himself.

"Well, you'll just have to figure something out. I'm not taking him," Marcus said.

Jacob huffed out a deep breath. "Fine. Could you feed him something this morning? There's not even a grain of salt in Raven's house."

"It's not Raven's anymore." Marcus scowled. "But yeah, I'll give you each a bowl of oatmeal. But that's it for the freebies. You want more, you work for it."

"I understand." Jacob ran his hand over his head. "What kind of work do you need done?"

9

P ain burned through Laura's foot as she awoke. She jerked into a sitting position, looking around wildly.

She saw a little glade filled with tall, dry grass, surrounded by cedars and cottonwoods. Her foot reminded her – of the earthquakes, the collapsed barn, the loss of her handful of possessions, the scary guy, the lost and found shoe, and especially the injured foot.

It needed attention, and quick. And now that it was daylight, she could see well enough to attend to it. And to see how bad it was.

Superficial scratches marred her toes and heel. A long scrape left a nasty red mark along the outside of her foot from her little toe to just below her ankle bone. That one stung a little.

The biggest concern was the bottom of her foot. A cut across her instep burned. The edges were red, and dirt was ground into it. Another slice, in her heel, also looked bad. It was moderately deep, and also had dirt and grass stains.

Her hands were scratched a little from her fall, but nothing there looked serious. The foot was a real problem.

She needed clean water, bandages, and antibiotic ointment at least. Oral antibiotics might be necessary, too.

It all seemed impossible, but she sent up a prayer, slid her shoe back on, and hobbled off on her walking stick. She returned to the highway, walking in the shaded areas as much as she could.

As she walked, she turned her thoughts to her children. Willow, tall and strong and beautiful, and Josh, becoming a good man like his dad. Were they waiting for her? At home? In Heaven? Out in the woods somewhere?

She had to keep going. Had to press on and find out what had become of them.

Bird calls filled the morning air. Robins, finches, even a bluebird. A faint smile curved her lips. They seemed to not have a care in the world. And yet, she knew, their Heavenly Father fed them, cared for them, and noticed when they released their final breath.

How much more did He care for her, His daughter Laura Archer? And her children, Willow and Josh?

Daisies danced in the morning sun, displaying their perfect white petals and brilliant yellow centers. Wild orange lilies bowed in the breeze as she walked by. She was reminded that the same Father clothed them in these beautiful colors.

How much more would He care for and clothe His own children?

She drew strength from focusing on the Father. Lifting her head, she saw a sparkle in the distance at the same moment a gurgling sound reached her ears.

Water! She hurried forward.

A laughing little brook rushed down the slope, splashing on mossy rocks before cascading into a shallow pool and then racing through a culvert under the highway and shooting out the far side.

Thank you, Lord! She lifted her eyes to heaven before hurrying forward to drink and wash in the brilliant, clear water.

Normally, she would have been cautious about drinking unfiltered mountain water, but God had sent this for her. She prayed over it before drinking, asking that it would bring health and healing to her body, and that any bacteria that might be in it would be bound up and not affect her in any bad way.

The cold water felt like liquid heaven in her parched throat.

She washed her face and neck, then slowly eased her feet into the cold stream. The water stung the cuts on her feet, but the pain eased after a few moments. She washed her right foot first, then turned her attention to the injured foot.

After she got it clean, she looked around for something to use as a bandage.

Finding nothing, she sighed. Putting an injured but clean foot into a dusty shoe was a bad plan. But what could she do?

She fingered the hem of her blue dress, and got an idea. It was cotton, so it was absorbent. Now, she just needed to tear off a strip along the bottom of the hem. Fortunately, it was a modest length, so losing an inch or two wouldn't be a problem.

WHEN WILLOW WALKED into the barn, Deborah and Jaci were milking Myth and Sassafras, while Beth and Delia looked on. The pygmy goat buckling, Buster, stamped his little feet and play-butted Beth, who laughed with delight.

"Thanks for taking care of the goats," Willow said to the women.

"We're watching and learning how to milk, too," Delia said.

"Yeah," her sister nodded. "Grandma said we should all learn how to do all the chores."

"Excellent idea." Willow glanced at Deborah. "Where are the guys?"

"Clark and Alan are removing brush from around the new cabin, like you suggested yesterday." She handed Willow the milk pail. "And the boys are hauling more water from the creek."

"Good." Willow went to the doorway. "I'd encourage you all to get packed today, with whatever you need to evacuate. We'll be doing the same."

"We don't have much stuff," Jaci said. "So that should be easy."

Willow smiled wanly. Well, maybe that was one benefit to being a refugee. Most of your belongings fit on your back.

Still, her group had accumulated some things since arriving at the cabin. Like the tools and expired but edible canned food that was already here, as well as the food and chickens the Andersons had sent over, plus the extra guns and ammo they'd recently picked up after the fight with the black-clad ninja men. Also, her group had made a couple trips to town for extra gear from home, and had bought chicken feed and whatnot. So their belongings could not all be carried in a single trip. Or even two.

They would have to prioritize. Select the most essential items, and pack those first. Then add whatever else they could carry. Plus the goats and chickens, of course.

Once they found a safe evacuation location, perhaps there would be time to return for the rest of their gear and food.

But what if there wasn't time for a second trip?

She frowned. They couldn't afford to lose anything! Each item was necessary for their survival through the fast-approaching winter.

Oh, dear God... please help us.

She looked south. Was that smoke plume getting larger? Or was it just her imagination?

As Willow approached the cabin, Raven came out the door.

"I have an idea!" Her long black hair floated loose around her shoulders, and Gilligan trotted beside her.

"I hope it's a great one." Willow glanced again toward the forest fire.

"We should stow some of our stuff in the creek!"

"What?" Willow's gaze ricocheted back to Raven.

"Think about it – things like tools, canned goods, maybe some extra clothes, whatever won't be wrecked by being in the water for a few days. If the fire comes this way, maybe they won't burn up."

"Tools and cans would rust."

"Even after just a few days?" Raven's smile faded. "Doesn't it have to be exposed to oxygen in order to rust?"

"I don't know. Old sunken ships are rusty."

"True. But we won't be able to carry everything. And we can't leave it here to burn."

"Yeah, I know." Willow scratched a mosquito bite on her arm.

"Hey!" Raven exclaimed. "What if we bury stuff?"

"Hmmm." Willow pursed her lips, then nodded. "That could work if it's deep enough, and far from tree roots. A fire can smolder through wood roots for a while."

Raven smiled. "Great! Let's get on it!"

Josh and Matt returned with buckets from the creek, which Jaci and Deborah used to water the chickens and goats. Afterwards, everyone spent some time preparing their evacuation packs. Willow mostly put survival necessities in hers, but she also wrapped her mom's wool sweater around her Bible after she tucked the family photos inside the front cover.

By mid-morning, the guys began digging a three-foot deep trench in the meadow behind the barn. Alan offered to let the group use his family's tarp to wrap items that needed to be protected from the soil. Clark wrapped extra clothes and the chicken feed in the tarp.

Raven, Willow and Candy brought tools and canned food to store in the trench. By noon, everything that wasn't going in someone's pack was carefully placed in the trench and covered with dirt. Josh and Matt packed the soil by walking over it repeatedly, with Delia and Beth happily joining in.

The smoke grew heavier as the afternoon wore on. Willow tried to see the smoke plume from the fire, but the grey stench was so thick, she could barely see the trees at the far end of the meadow, much less the Andersons' ridge or any of the nearest mountain slopes.

Everyone hauled water during the afternoon, and they soaked the barn and cabin roofs and the new cabin. Finally, they watered the garden once again.

Willow gathered everyone for another dinner of real spaghetti, compliments of their friends the Andersons.

Surely John and Jeannie and their friends had left their retreat by now. And they had not come north to join Willow's group, so they must have gone into town. Or perhaps they'd taken shelter in the vacant home down the road from their place, where they'd driven out the evil men in black. That house might be out of the way of the fire. It could be a perfect fallback location – depending on the fire's movements, of course.

Alan prayed a blessing over the food, and prayed for protection for the Andersons' group and their own. He also prayed for Uncle Tony, wherever he was.

Then they feasted.

Willow couldn't know what would happen tomorrow, but she was grateful for all that was accomplished today. And she figured a meal of heavy starches would provide the energy that everyone was likely to need for a big trek in the morning.

As she savored her last bite of the tasty pasta, she looked

toward the garden. It was going gangbusters in the rich soil and long, sunny days. But left alone, it would quickly wither and die, and with it, the group's hopes for survival this winter.

But what could they do?

Maybe she was wrong, but it seemed like their choices were devastatingly bad: stay to save the garden, and possibly die in the wildfire; or run to escape the fire, and face starvation in the coming winter.

They would discuss it again tonight, continue praying for direction, and make the final call in the morning.

She carried her plate to Raven, who was beginning to wash the dinner dishes. Candy brought her plate and Maria's. She leaned close to Willow.

"Can I talk to you?" she whispered. Her expression was earnest and intense. "Someplace... private?"

"About what?" Willow asked, not bothering to lower her voice.

"Maria." She glanced around furtively.

Willow shrugged, even as her stomach began to turn. "Sure. Let's go out to the garden."

Candy nodded and picked up her daughter, then strode out to the hilled potatoes.

Willow followed. So – Candy was going to admit what Willow already knew – she'd had an affair with Willow's dad, and Maria was their love child. Then Willow would have to forgive her... again. Like she'd been doing every day since –

"Look, I already know," Willow blurted.

"What?" Bewilderment, then fear, flickered in Candy's eyes.

"About Maria." Willow stared at her.

"Ah... uh..." Candy moved Maria to her other hip. Her gaze darted around, like a trapped bird seeking escape from a snare.

"That's not what you wanted to talk about?" Willow pressed. "You said you wanted to talk about her."

Candy gulped. "Um, well..."

The girl squirmed, and Candy set her down. "Stay out of the potatoes."

Finally, she met Willow's gaze.

"I, uh, wanted to talk to you about who'd take care of her. If anything happened to me."

Willow didn't respond. This conversation was not going where she'd expected. So she'd let Candy carry it.

"But you *know?*" Candy's lip quivered. Her blue eyes filled with tears, but didn't they spill.

Willow nodded.

"How long?" Candy whispered.

"Since I found your texts in Dad's phone. Not long after he died." Now tears rushed to her own eyes.

"I'm sorry!" Candy's hands covered her mouth. The tears began to fall. She hung her head. "I'm so sorry."

"Hey." Tears choked her voice. "Look at me."

Candy raised her head and peered at Willow with flooded eyes. She wiped them with her hands.

"I forgive you," Willow whispered. "And when I get mad, I forgive you again."

"*How?*" Candy sobbed. "I can't even forgive me!"

"I give it to God. I let it go."

"Just like that?" Candy's reddened eyes searched Willow's. "It's that easy?"

"Yes." She paused. "And that difficult."

JACOB AGREED to subcontract one of Marcus's night shifts guarding a local farm, and talked Heidi into babysitting Danny overnight in return for breakfast when he picked the kid up in the morning.

In exchange for the shift, Marcus promised to supply Jacob with enough food for him and Danny for one day.

Jacob wasn't sure this was a fair wage, and he wasn't sure how much the farmer was actually paying Marcus. But he needed to eat. And so did the kid.

Of course, since he was paying one meal to Heidi, he only got two for himself. But he could survive on that for now, until he sorted things out.

The farmer, Chad Litton, gave him a shooting test. It was too easy. Three rifle rounds into a five-inch target at fifty yards. And the rifle had a scope!

After that, the farmer was happy, and turned Jacob loose to guard the perimeter and entrance to the farm. So far, it was the most boring job he'd ever had.

It gave him too much time to think.

Night deepened as he walked the farmer's fence line, eyes and ears alert, but mind focused on his own problems.

For the life of him, Jacob could not figure out what to do about Danny. Back when things were normal, it wouldn't have been a question. The state would have sheltered the kid, then put him into foster care or something.

Did he have grandparents? Aunts or uncles nearby? Heidi had said she wasn't aware of any relatives in Ponderosa.

And Danny wasn't much help. He said he had a grandma. And she lived at the ocean. Well, there were no oceans in Montana, so he wouldn't be going to live with her.

Jacob had gone through all the paperwork he'd found at Danny's home. There were a few postcards from Oregon, but not much else. No letters, no cards, no addresses. Everything was electronic these days – or had been, until a couple weeks ago when the EMP hit.

The neighbors had buried Danny's mom already. Jacob searched the house for a will or anything that might have indicated her wishes for who would become Danny's guardian if she died. He came up dry.

Surely there was someone who cared about the kid and would take him in. Or at least someone who would take pity on him and give him a home.

Jacob reached the northwest corner of the property and turned east along the north fence. The moon was bright enough he didn't bother with a flashlight. It would give away his position, anyway, if anybody was skulking around.

Orphans had existed throughout human history. The government foster system was relatively new. Who had taken those kids in and raised them all the previous millennia?

Churches, right? The same people who originally built and staffed the schools, universities and hospitals before businesses and governments took over those services. They also ran orphanages.

Well, that's where he would go, then. He'd take the kid to church and find a home for him among the faithful few.

Something about this idea rubbed him wrong, but he shook it off.

He had to find a home for Danny. There was no way he could care for the kid himself.

The moon illuminated the white tops of the green metal fence posts as he walked the east side of the 40-acre farm. Fortunately, it was only about a mile to town, so it didn't take too long to get out here, or to get back to Heidi's place to pick up the kid.

He was lucky it was a small farm. He'd hate to be responsible for patrolling a 200-acre farm alone in the dark. The Litton family had a few barnyard animals, including ducks, sheep and three pigs. The bulk of the farm was a big potato patch. If they had a decent crop and stored it properly, they'd be set all winter. Provided the potatoes weren't stolen, of course. Or the Littons weren't killed for their food.

But that's what Jacob was here for – to make sure that didn't happen. At least, not at night.

He wasn't sure what their arrangement was during the daylight hours.

Yawning, he glanced east as he reached the southern property line. Eventually that horizon would lighten, signaling a new day and the end of his shift.

As soon as she saw the faintest light through the window, Willow climbed out of her bunk and put on her boots. Her head ached. She'd barely slept, trying to find other options for escaping the fire and saving the garden. It was too early to harvest very much. The carrots, potatoes and tomatoes wouldn't be ready for a while.

She hurried to the door and walked outside. The low-lying smoke had cleared a bit overnight, and now she could clearly see the huge plume to the south.

She gulped.

The whole ridge was ablaze!

In the predawn light, the trees along the top of the Andersons' ridge flamed like eighty-foot-tall orange and red torches. There was no way their home and barn had survived. Those buildings were probably ablaze right now.

A breeze blew her hair off her shoulders. A stiff breeze. From the south.

Dear Lord. That monster was coming, and that wind was blowing it straight at them!

She swallowed past the dry lump in her throat, then whirled and raced into the cabin.

"Everybody up! Now!"

As the dwelling came alive with grunts, murmurs and questions, Willow gave orders.

"Get dressed. The fire's coming! Roll up your bedding and put it with your packs! Boys, you go take care of the goats and chickens. Raven, would you start breakfast? Candy, make sure Maria is ready to go." She took a breath. "I'm going to the new cabin to get the others."

With that, she raced around the cabin, up the hill to the new family's home, and pounded on the door. Gilligan followed, barking.

Moments later, Jaci opened the door, fully dressed except her shoes.

"Get ready as quick as you can! The fire is coming over the ridge."

Jaci's mouth slackened. "Oh, no."

"I think we'll have to evacuate. Get all your gear, and come down for breakfast."

Willow hurried back down the hill. The boys were walking to the barn, and she urged them to milk the goats first. After breakfast, they'd have to round up the chickens and put them in the boxes and little crates they'd carried them in when they first arrived here.

It felt like such a huge loss.

Why had God brought them here, to this perfect old homestead, let them work hard to improve the barn, put in a garden and build a second cabin, only to let it all be destroyed before winter?

They were back where they started when they fled Ponderosa. Actually, they were worse off now, because they had even less time to prepare before the perils of winter arrived.

There was no way they could start a new garden this late in the summer, much less build a home and barn without real tools, boards or nails.

Despair flooded her spirit. She turned again to stare at the massive forest fire.

Then she put on a brave face and entered the cabin. Perhaps for the last time.

JACOB STRETCHED AND YAWNED. The sun was about to break over the eastern mountains, signaling the end of his first shift. He glanced toward Willow's Wilderness, then rubbed his eyes to be sure he was really seeing what he thought he saw.

A thick column of smoke rose from the mountains. A wildfire! And by the looks of it, a big, hot one.

Why hadn't he noticed it before?

He'd been busy in town, for sure, after the earthquakes and taking care of Danny and getting a night job. Maybe the smoke from the city fires had obscured the view south toward Raven and Willow's hideout yesterday.

Should he do something? Go warn them?

Surely they could see it themselves. And if he knew those girls, they'd been monitoring it and making plans.

But did they realize how devastating it could be? How quickly it could move?

They were country girls. They should know. Right?

He had worked wildfires for two seasons in college, and that was enough. It was hard, dirty, hot and tedious work. Not to mention dangerous.

But he'd learned a lot doing it. Mostly about how unpredictable a fire could be. How fast it could run. How terrifying it could sound. How deadly it could turn.

He scratched a gnat bite on his bicep.

He should go warn them. Go help them.

But how? It was miles back to their mountain. It'd take all day to hike back there. By then, it could be too late.

In fact, they might have left already. They probably had. Almost certainly had.

Where would they go?

Would they return to town? Find him in Raven's house? How would he explain that?

He picked up a pebble and chucked it at a fence post.

Thunk! The pebble bounced back at him.

Of course they would go to Raven's house. Or possibly Willow and Josh's place. Where else would they go? Their friends, the Andersons, maybe? That would be a good choice. The only obvious one, as far as he knew.

But what did he know? They might have a half-dozen good choices. They'd lived here a long time, knew a lot of people.

Nah... if they had a selection of good choices, they wouldn't have to be scraping a living out of the wilderness. As Christians, their options were extremely limited. They'd probably joined the Andersons at their retreat. A real nice place.

Anyway, the sun was up. His shift was over.

He couldn't go help them if he wanted to. He had to go pick up Danny from Heidi's place.

And see about pawning the kid off on some church folks.

Jacob walked to the house to leave the farmer's rifle on the covered front porch as he'd been instructed. He'd never mentioned that he had his own AR-15. Or Glock 17.

Over the years, he'd learned to keep his mouth shut about anything that mattered. And he'd learned at a very early age that guns mattered. So he collected a couple, took good care of them, and kept mum about them.

He double-checked the safety before leaning the rifle up

against the wall. As he turned toward the road, he noticed movement. He paused, his back against the house and his left hand reaching toward the rifle barrel.

Trees along the property line obscured his view.

Was somebody on the farm property?

Or were they on the county road?

WILLOW'S FRIENDS had prayed about it, and they were all on board for evacuating – especially as they watched the blazing inferno consuming the trees on the Andersons' ridge. Still, she wanted to make sure everyone fully understood the consequences of leaving the homestead.

"We might be able to come back, but the garden will be lost," she glanced from Alan to Clark, then to their wives. "That was supposed to provide a lot of our food this fall and winter. Without it..."

Her unfinished sentence hung in the air.

"We sure can't stay here!" Candy scooped up her daughter. "We'll burn alive!"

"Perhaps one of us should stay." Clark spoke slowly. "To mind the garden."

"No!" Jaci grabbed her husband's arm, fear in her eyes. "I can see what you're thinking. Don't. The girls and I – we need you!"

Her eyes grew round and teary.

"We have to stay together!"

"I could stay." Alan's voice was hoarse. "The fire might not even come here. We might let the garden be lost for nothing!"

"If you stay, I stay," Deborah said.

"No. That's too dangerous."

"I won't leave you." She took her husband's hand. "Not now. Not ever."

Finally, Raven spoke up.

"I've prayed about this, a lot. I believe that God will make a way for us to get through the winter. But today, we need to evacuate. All of us." She looked around the group. "Did any of you hear anything different in your prayer time?"

There were some downcast eyes, and some heads shook.

"Okay." Willow reached for her pack. "I think that settles it. Let's pray over this place before we leave. Who wants to do the honors?"

"I will." Raven volunteered, and prayed a power prayer over their little homestead. She asked for a miracle for the garden, and protection over all the buildings, trees and land.

As Raven prayed, Willow felt her faith and courage blossom. God had taken care of them in the past. He would do the same in the future. And one day, soon, they would see Him. That day, no matter what else had happened, would be the best day of their entire lives.

THE JUST-RISEN sun was in Jacob's eyes as he tried to make out what was happening along the property line. His hand grabbed the rifle barrel. Squinting, he pulled the gun to him and raised it.

Careful to keep the sun's rays out of his line of sight, he looked through the scope. No good. The sun was right there. He lowered the weapon and shielded his eyes with his hand.

As best he could tell, the people were on the road's right of way, not the farm property.

They were probably travelers. It looked like four adults. And some animals.

Had they stolen them?

Not from this farm, he was sure of that. Plus, his shift was over. He set the rifle against the wall of the house and slowly started toward the road, making a point of staying in the shadows of the trees as he walked.

The travelers were moving towards town, leading a couple of horses and a couple of cows. All loaded down with big packs.

Jacob let them get a good distance ahead of him before he walked off the farm onto the county road. He had plenty of time before he had to pick up Danny. So he trailed them by a couple hundred yards.

They were moving along at a pretty good clip, given the stock animals and the heavy packs. Maybe they were running from something. Maybe they wanted to get out the far side of town before the world was awake.

Maybe he'd follow them a bit and see where they were going.

In about fifteen minutes, they reached the outskirts of town. They continued straight along the highway. If they didn't turn off, they'd soon reach Marcus's neighborhood, then pass by Raven's.

Eventually, the road continued on north, out of Ponderosa. After that, the highway hit a few more small towns, miles apart, and eventually came to the Canadian border.

Was the border still open? Maybe that's where these folks were going.

Maybe he should go there, too. What if the EMP hadn't hit Canada as hard? What if more of their infrastructure and food production systems were still functional? He could slip across the border. Once he found a home for Danny.

Jacob sauntered along, far behind the travelers, making a point of staying on the east side of the road where he could best blend into the morning's shadows.

He should swing by Marcus's place to pick up his meals for

the day. But these travelers were intriguing, and he considered following them a while longer. Besides, it was really early. Danny would probably still be sleeping. And maybe Heidi was, too.

He had time to kill.

11

Jacob stayed a good distance behind the travelers, who continued on the road past Marcus's neighborhood. A few times, he had to pick up his pace to keep up with theirs. They definitely seemed to be in a hurry, which piqued his curiosity even more.

Were they thieves? Or were they worried that someone would steal their own animals? Or was there some other reason they seemed to be in a rush?

Maybe they didn't have the I.D. chip!

The guy in front turned around and looked back, and Jacob stepped behind an oak tree.

Then the leader continued through the next intersection. They were almost to Raven's road now.

He'd follow them a bit further, then maybe watch and see if they left town. Then he'd hustle back to Marcus's house, get his food, and go pick up Danny.

But when they got to Raven's road, they stopped. The leader looked up, then gestured at the street sign.

Then they started down her road! *His* road!

What had been casual curiosity now turned to concern.

Who were these sneaky, hurried people, and why were they going down this little country road? It didn't really go anywhere. It dead ended at some farms at the base of the mountains.

Plus, since they'd turned off the main road, he couldn't see them! Homes and trees blocked his view.

He'd have to hustle to get to that intersection himself, so he could see what they were doing. Or where they might stop.

Maybe he was being stupid. Maybe they knew someone here. Or maybe they lived at one of the farms at the end of the road.

It really wasn't any of his business what they were up to, but since he lived here, for the time being, anyway, he wanted to know. So he broke into a jog.

When he reached the last house before the intersection, he slowed and shifted into a saunter. If they were still looking back, he wanted to look casual. Not raise alarms.

He scanned through the chain link fence of the yard at the corner. Didn't see them.

Easing up to the intersection, he looked down the road.

The group had stopped, near Raven's house, and both men were looking back.

He'd been spotted.

WILLOW LED HER GROUP NORTH, in the general direction of Ponderosa. They wouldn't enter town, of course. That was too dangerous.

When they got far enough away from the fire, they'd find a place to hunker down. Maybe they'd send a scout back every so often to check on the location and progress of the fire. Raven was the obvious choice for this, because she was a marathoner.

But she wasn't that great at directions. What if she got lost? What if she couldn't find her way back to the group?

Willow couldn't bear the thought of losing her. She couldn't bear the thought of losing anyone. But especially not Raven, who'd become her best friend and her confidant.

Maybe she and Raven could scout together.

Willow's sense of direction had always been good, and she was careful about noticing landmarks. Yeah, she'd gotten a little lost that first night they'd left Ponderosa, but that was in the dark. And she'd eventually found the dirt road she was looking for – before Matt and Josh realized she actually *was* lost.

As they crossed a meadow, Candy came up beside her, carrying Maria.

"Where are we going?"

"I'm not sure yet."

"I hope we're not just going to wander around for weeks, like before."

Willow rolled her eyes, but said nothing. Despite their tearful conversation last night, Candy hadn't changed. That woman had a way of getting on everyone's nerves. How could anyone like her?

She remembered the Bible verse about loving her enemies. And she was trying. Truly, she was.

But *loving* was not the same as *liking*.

Raven caught up to them, with Gilligan at her heels. She glanced over her shoulder.

"Man, this smoke is bad!"

"I've been gagging on it all morning," Willow said, glad for the distraction.

"It makes my hair reek." Candy swung her head, tossing her blonde curls over her shoulder. "It smells like I've been in a bar."

Willow shot her a pointed look. "I wouldn't know."

"It's not like I was a bar fly!" Candy's words were rushed. "I've just gone occasionally, and all the cigarettes stink up my hair."

"You won't have that problem anymore." Raven reached down to pet Gilligan's shoulders. "And maybe we can all wash our hair when we stop for the night."

Always the peacemaker. Willow glanced at her friend before stepping over a downed log. Raven had a knack for diplomacy. One that she herself would probably never learn. Perhaps she could work on it. What was that verse? A soft answer turns away wrath? Raven almost always had a soft answer.

It's why everyone loved Raven.

"Huckabears!" Maria squealed and pointed.

The little tot was right. Off to the left, on a short, sunny slope, grew a nice patch of huckleberries.

"Let's take a break," Willow said.

"Looks like somebody was paying attention in foraging class!" Raven helped Maria pick some of the berries. "Only pick the dark ones. They're ripe."

The group scattered into the patch, searching for the biggest, ripest berries.

Willow tossed three in her mouth and slowly crushed them. Sweet, sour flavor exploded on her tongue, making her mouth water even more. She lifted the branches of the nearest bush to reveal a bountiful harvest under the foliage.

Fingering them off their bush, she ate as fast as she picked. Oh, the deliciousness!

She paused and looked up. Everyone was harvesting and eating the luscious purple berries. The mid-morning sun looked weirdly orange through the forest fire smoke. She went back to plucking and eating.

It was a perfect break and snack. Prepared by God, months ago. He'd known they'd come by here on this sad day, and enjoy this bounty.

She turned her face toward the sky and whispered her gratefulness for His goodness.

After a few minutes, the best berries were consumed and the group looked happy, their fingertips and tongues stained purple.

"Let's all pick a little more for tonight," Willow said. "We'll be glad to have them this evening."

They spent another five minutes harvesting, and they collected all the berries in a bag, which Raven placed in the top of her pack so they wouldn't get crushed.

"Okay, gang, let's get going." Willow led the way down a deer trail. It meandered crookedly along the hillside, like most game trails, but it was easier to follow than to break a new trail through the trees.

The mountain air grew warm as noon approached, then muggy in the afternoon. The temperature and humidity sapped her energy. The group stopped beside a creek for a break.

Willow plunged her arms into the clear water, then splashed some on her hot face.

It would be great to take a nice, long nap right here in the shade. Dangling her feet in the cool mountain stream.

The smoky air made her sneeze. Twice.

"Bless you," Deborah said, splashing water on her arms.

"Thanks. I'll be glad to get away from this smoke."

"I'm sure it's bad for our lungs." She glanced toward her husband. Alan knelt by the stream and dunked his head under water.

"Maybe we'll find a place where it's not so bad tonight." Willow rose to her feet. "We have to keep going."

"Hey." Raven touched her arm, then pointed west. "Check that out."

Tall, puffy clouds were forming beyond the mountain range.

"Maybe we'll get rain," Candy said. "And it'll put out the fire!"

"I wouldn't count on it." Raven gazed at the clouds. "With this kind of day, we're likely to have thunderstorms."

JACOB WOKE up from his nap with a start. What time was it? Where was the kid?

He rubbed his eyes and sat up. The hot, muggy afternoon felt oppressive. He lowered his feet to the floor and went to check on Danny.

He'd told him to stay in the house. Had he managed that? Or had he, like a young Jacob, been too captivated by the call of the outdoors – the bugs, the bees, the birds and trees? There was one perfect for climbing in Raven's backyard.

Was Danny old enough to be a tree climber?

The kid wasn't upstairs, so Jacob went down to the living room. It wasn't like there were any toys or books of interest to a four year old in this house.

He found the kid in the dining room. He'd found a sheet, probably in Raven's linen closet, and had draped it over two chairs.

"I'm camping!" Danny announced as Jacob lifted a corner of the sheet. "This is my tent! Do you wanna come in?"

Jacob rocked back on his heels.

"I don't think I'd fit in there."

"Yes, you will." Danny scooted back into the far corner. "There's room. C'mon!"

"Nah, that's okay." Jacob stood up. "Why are the pots and pans on the floor?"

"I told you! I'm camping." Danny hustled out from under his makeshift tent. He pointed at the fry pan. "That's pancakes!"

"Hmmm." Jacob looked at the empty pan. The kid had some imagination. "What's in that pot?"

"It's mac'n cheese! With ketchup."

Macaroni and cheese, with ketchup? Sounded awful. Jacob eyed the kid.

"Okay, you enjoy that. I'm going to get some rest." He turned and started out of the kitchen.

"Can't we do something fun?"

Jacob glanced back. He'd been up all night. He was exhausted. And he'd be up all night tonight, too. Then tomorrow, he had to find a church family to take in Danny.

"I can't, buddy. I'm too tired."

Disappointment clouded Danny's eyes. A frown puckered his lips.

"I want my mom!"

Oh, man. Jacob grimaced. He was too tired for this.

Danny's frown turned into a sob as his eyes grew teary. He sat beside his tent, his knees tucked up to his chest, his arms wrapped around his legs. He lowered his face to his knees and cried.

"Hey." Jacob's voice was weak. He swallowed and tried again, putting his hand on the kid's back. "How about if we go out in the yard for a while?"

Danny looked up, snotty nosed and snuffling. Slowly, he nodded. Then he reached for Jacob's hand.

Jacob led him to the back door.

"Here's the deal – I'll be here on the porch. You have to stay where you can see me." He stared into the kid's eyes. "Got it?"

Danny let go of his hand and sprinted for the nearest tree.

"And don't climb any trees!"

Jacob lowered himself to the porch swing. He had to get some rest. He'd slept – maybe – two hours since yesterday. He'd be on watch again tonight.

He got off the swing and stretched out on the shady porch, pulling down a cushion to use as a pillow. If the kid obeyed and stayed within sight of Jacob, he'd probably be just fine. If he disobeyed, well, that was his own fault, wasn't it? Jacob never intended to be his babysitter anyway.

Closing his eyes, his thoughts drifted back to the strange events of the morning.

The group he'd followed into town had been near enough to make out general descriptions – male/female, tall/short, and clothing color – but too far to make out hair color, age, or any identifying details.

When they'd spotted him, he'd made a point of casually crossing the road and moving on past the next house. He did cut through the nearest alley, though, so he could double back and see what they were doing.

They were still in front of Raven's driveway, and he was prepared to confront them, but they apparently held a mini-conference, complete with gestures, and then continued down the road.

He'd made his way to Raven's house, and hustled upstairs to the window at the end of the hall where he'd have the best vantage point to watch them without being seen himself.

They'd gone a bit further down the road, but he'd lost view of them through the foliage of the neighborhood trees. He'd wanted to wait a while to see if they came back, but he was out of time. He was late to pick up Danny, and he had to run to Marcus's place first to get food.

So he'd rushed off to do all that.

Jacob yawned and glanced over at Danny, who was playing with a short stick at the base of a weeping willow. He closed his eyes and fell into oblivion.

$\sim$

THE SKY GREW DARKER as Willow and her group continued hiking north.

She cast a concerned glance to the west. The clouds were gathering and approaching. Tall, dark and ominous.

And then she heard it – the rumble of thunder. She stopped and waited for everyone to catch up to her. Thunder rolled again in the distance.

"We need to find a spot to ride out the storm." She studied the clouds. "When you hear thunder, you're close enough to the storm to get hit by lightning."

"Where should we go?" Jaci's sweet face creased with concern as she wrapped an arm around Beth's shoulders. The girl looked up at her mom and leaned in.

"We don't want to be under any tall trees, or out in the open," Willow said.

"Right, and not on any hilltops," Raven added. "Better to be in a low spot, maybe under some short trees."

"So let's make our way downhill, and look for a place with young trees." Willow glanced at her friends. "And spread out a little. Keep at least thirty feet between you and the person ahead of you."

"Why?" Candy asked. "What about Maria?"

"It's just a precaution to prevent multiple people from being hit by a single lightning strike. But you can keep Maria with you."

The first low spot they came across had a creek running through it.

"No good," Raven said. "We need a dry location."

As they pressed on, the wind picked up, swaying the trees around them. From the corner of her eye, Willow saw a bright flash. She began counting off seconds, and thunder boomed when she reached twenty-five.

"That one was only about five miles away!" She picked up

her pace. "We need to hurry."

Smoke burned her eyes as she hiked through timber at the crest of a small hill. But the air was cooling dramatically as the thunderhead blocked out more of the sunlight. A drop of rain hit her forehead, then another one splatted on her arm.

Lightning flashed across the mountaintop west of her. She only got to thirteen before the thunder rolled. That was two or three miles. They needed to hunker down, and fast.

She hurried downslope under the cover of tall pines and firs. About a hundred yards ahead, she spied an area where a small wildfire had burned through. The tall trees were gone, and younger trees had taken their place. The tallest ones appeared to be about twenty feet in height.

"That looks good!" Willow motioned toward the spot. Thunder drowned out her words. "Hurry!"

As the group reached the low area, Raven reminded everyone to spread out.

"Try to stay thirty feet apart, or more!" Her voice carried over the whipping wind. "Take off your backpacks and set them far away from you. Those animal kennels have metal mesh – keep them away from each other, and away from yourselves!"

Willow took over from there, as the wind whipped her hair.

"If your skin tingles or your hair stands on end, get into the lightning squat. Like this!"

She demonstrated, squatting on the balls of her feet, heels together, hunched over her knees with her hands over her ears.

Matt laughed. "Is that supposed to keep you from getting struck?"

"Of course not! But it could help lightning to flow over you instead of instantly frying your internal organs."

"It looks ridiculous," Delia giggled. Lightning flashed across the forest they'd just hiked through, and thunder crashed over them. Delia dropped into the crouch, clapping her hands over her ears.

"Don't lie down," Raven instructed. "That makes a bigger target."

"I don't think I can hold that crouch position very long," Deborah said. "Maybe I'll just kneel."

"And pray!" Raven said, before telling Gilligan to sit. He cowered near a little tree, his ears pinned against his head, and tail tucked over his feet.

The wind grew fiercer, swaying the forest as Willow squatted down and watched lightning flash through the sky.

Maybe it would rain. She'd felt a few drops. Was that all they were getting? They needed rain. The forest needed it.

And now, as lightning filled the air around them, rain was necessary to put out any new fires caused by the lightning. But it didn't look like rain was on the agenda. Just wind, and bright flashes and thunder so loud it hurt her ears.

She glanced around at her friends. They'd spread out and hunkered down.

Gilligan flopped down on his belly and put his head on the ground, his eyes constantly watching Raven. The goats, tethered to very small trees, stomped their feet and pulled against their tethers. The chickens, in their various crates and boxes, were scattered around the area. They squawked their fear at the menacing storm.

It was bad, being caught outdoors in a storm like this. But her group had done their best to be as safe as possible. The rest was up to God. She looked skyward.

Lightning flashed almost directly overhead, and the thunder that followed a moment later deafened her. She screamed, and she wasn't the only one.

12

Jacob woke in a panic as a cannon thundered in the distance. He sat up, his back and hips sore from the porch boards. No, not a cannon. Just thunder.

As he stood up, lightning flashed across the street, and the resulting thunder assaulted his eardrums. Rain mixed with hail suddenly pinged off the metal roof. Within seconds, there was a deluge coming down.

Lightning flashed again. He needed to get inside.

Where was Danny?

His eyes scanned the yard. Nothing. The trees. Nothing. Maybe he'd had the good sense to go inside as the storm approached.

Jacob went through the door and closed it behind him as thunder boomed.

"Danny?" He walked through the kitchen, then glanced into the living room. Huh. Upstairs, maybe?

He took the stairs two at a time.

"Danny? Where are you?"

No answer.

He dashed through Raven's bedroom, the bathroom and the guest room. Danny wasn't here!

Maybe he was afraid and hid under the bed, or in the closet.

Jacob searched quickly, calling the kid's name the whole time. Nothing. Where could he be?

Lightning lit up the whole floor, followed by a terrible crashing explosion. It must have hit the house!

Or the tree or electric pole right outside.

His heart thudded.

Where was that kid?

He raced downstairs. Lightning flashed, illuminating the living room like paparazzi cameras. He covered his eyes as the thunder hammered his ears.

"Danny? DANNY!"

He ran toward the dining room table, where Danny had set up his sheet-and-chair tent. He must be hiding under there!

Jacob grabbed the corner of the sheet and yanked it back. It gave easily, flying off the chair and settling on the floor.

But Danny wasn't there.

He was gone.

WILLOW PRAYED for rain in the forest, but it didn't come. Just more wind, more lightning, and the terrifying concussions of thunder.

A particularly strong gust plastered her hair across her eyes and mouth.

CRACK! BOOM! BOOM! BOOM!

She raked her hair off her face with her fingers. One of the huge, swaying firs had snapped off about halfway up and crashed to the forest floor below.

She scanned her friends. Josh was nearest, by her design. She tried to stay close to her brother. He sat on the ground, huddled with his head low and tucked against the wind, hands over his ears.

Beyond him, Raven sat, her jet-black hair blowing at crazy angles around her head. Clark's family kneeled in a circle with his in-laws, but they all remained about twenty feet from each other. Matt sat on the periphery of that group, near the girls.

Off to one side sat Candy and Maria, a few feet away from each other.

The gusting wind stilled for a moment, and Willow's heart nearly stopped.

Little Maria's soft, fine hair was rising away from her head. Her tiny body was sending electric signals to the storm. Positive streamers.

She'd just become a lightning rod!

Willow stared in horror as Maria's hair stood on end, reaching toward the sky.

What could she do? Nothing. But beg for mercy.

Dear God, dear God, dear God!

Finally, she found her voice.

"Maria!" She yelled over the wind. "Put your hands over your ears!"

Candy's eyes had been closed against the wind, but now they opened and stared at her daughter, a half dozen feet away from her.

Instantly, she was on her feet, moving toward Maria.

"Nooooo!" Willow yelled. "Get back!"

But Candy's arms wrapped around her child, her body folding over her like a shield.

Suddenly, the air crackled.

Time slowed as Willow's skin tingled. She decided to close her eyes, but couldn't do it.

Like watching a movie frame by frame, a brilliant flash filled the air, zapping trees and searing her retinas.

And then, the explosion of thunder, like a bomb going off in front of her. Heat warming her skin. The smell of burning, cooking, searing singed clothing. Or was it flesh?

LIGHT FLASHED through the dining room window, illuminating the white sheet Danny had used for his makeshift tent.

Thunder crashed over Jacob moments later.

The huge storm was right on top of them!

Where could Danny be?

Jacob took a step toward the window and looked out. A roar filled the house as hailstones the size of nickels hammered the roof and pelted the walkway outside.

The kid wasn't really out there, was he?

But he sure wasn't in here!

Perhaps he'd gotten inside a shed, or crawled into a car.

He was four – old enough to get out of the storm.

Anyway, Jacob couldn't go outside to look for him now. He saw hailstones that were bigger now – the size of quarters – pounding the yard.

The old house had a metal roof, and the sound was deafening.

But eventually it would stop. He'd look for the kid when it let up.

An ear-splitting crack filled the air as lightning hit a tree just across the road. Almost simultaneously, thunder answered with its deafening, crashing boom.

His heart thumped, missing a beat, feeling like it flip-flopped in his chest.

He took a deep breath and exhaled through his mouth. He needed a clear head. He had to think!

But what was there to decide?

The choices were plain: stay inside and stay alive, or go outside in a deadly storm and probably get killed.

It was a no-brainer.

He reached for his hat.

WILLOW BLINKED, then blinked again. If felt as if the lightning had fried her vision, like she'd looked at the sun. But slowly things began coming into focus.

Trees. People. Gilligan, a black and white blob, running toward Candy and Maria.

Rain hit her head. A few big, fat drops. The smell of singed hair burned her nose.

Candy lay sprawled on the ground next to her daughter.

Maria began shrieking. She sat up and reached for her mom's arm.

Willow felt herself propelled to her feet, moving toward the pair.

Lightning flashed. Thunder crashed.

Willow tumbled to the ground. She was halfway to them. She started crawling on her hands and knees. The rain hit hard then, like someone had turned on a faucet. It plastered her hair to her head.

Another bolt of lightning hit a tall tree less than a hundred yards away. She cringed, but kept moving. Pine cones poked her palms as she scrambled toward Candy and the child.

"Candy!" Finally she reached her. "Candy!"

Her eyes were closed. Her face, motionless.

Was she even breathing?

Dear God! Dear God!

Willow grabbed her wrist. A pulse?

She felt nothing.

Didn't see any rise or fall of Candy's chest.

She pressed her fingers into Candy's throat, searching for her carotid artery. Maybe she could find a pulse?

Rain drenched her back and shoulders as she knelt over the woman, Maria wailing at her elbow.

Suddenly, Raven was at her side. Then Clark, and Deborah, and Alan.

"Split up! Back away!" She motioned them away from her.

Folklore said lightning didn't hit the same place twice, but she knew it wasn't true. The Empire State Building got struck dozens of times a year.

Deborah scooped up Maria and moved away with the others.

"I'm staying," Raven yelled over the wind. "I'll help!"

"I can't find her pulse!" Willow stared at her friend. "She's not breathing!"

"Okay, CPR!" Raven scrambled around Candy, kneeling near her shoulder. "You do compressions!"

Raven checked and cleared Candy's airway, tilting her head back and her chin up, before Willow began counting off chest compressions.

The rain turned to hail, pelting her head and shoulders. She paused for Raven to blow air into Candy's lungs.

The hail stung her head and back as she continued. While Raven gave Candy air, Willow felt her wrist again.

"We have a pulse!" She yelled.

Raven's fingers flew to Candy's throat. After a moment, she nodded.

"It's weak and erratic." Raven stared at Candy's chest. "Is she breathing?"

Willow watched, but didn't see any rise or fall. She placed

her fingers in front of Candy's nose and mouth. Felt no air movement from her.

"I don't think so!"

"I'll keep going with the resuscitation." Raven pinched Candy's nose closed and blew more air into her lungs.

Lightning flashed on the hilltop, followed by rumbling thunder.

Willow sat back on her heels. Her friends were still scattered around the area, cowering under the assault of rain and hail.

Candy's clothing smelled singed. A leg of her jeans had a burn hole in it. One of her shoes was upside down, maybe ten feet away.

Blown clear off her body.

LAURA HOBBLED along the side of the highway, leaning on her walking stick. Her foot ached. She'd tried to keep it as clean as she could, but she could feel dust in her shoes, between her toes and under her heels.

There was no way to keep it clean. Not if she was going to walk home.

And she was definitely walking. Even during the day sometimes, like now.

She'd rested during the hottest part of the day, but in the late afternoon, sometimes the air cooled. Far ahead, in the distance, she spotted a massive anvil cloud.

A huge thunderhead.

Somebody was getting a lot of weather up there, and it didn't look nice.

But it was a good ten miles ahead of her, at least. Probably fifteen.

She was getting close to home now. So close she could almost taste it.

Another mile, and she'd be in her home county. Sixteen miles further, she'd reach the outskirts of Ponderosa.

At last.

There'd been times when she'd thought she wouldn't make it. Many times, actually.

She wasn't even hungry anymore. She'd gone so long without a good meal, maybe her stomach had shut down or something.

Whenever she could find something edible, she'd eat it, of course.

But nobody was offering handouts to the handful of travelers wandering up the roads. She sensed the small towns growing increasingly hostile. It was understandable. They didn't have food for themselves, much less to share.

Also, they were suspicious of strangers. With good reason – she'd been sorely tempted to steal, and many others probably had done so.

Where she had been slender and fit two months ago, she was now emaciated. Her ribs protruded, her arms were skinny. She imagined her face was gaunt. She hadn't had much extra weight to lose, so losing any was detrimental to her. She had no fat reserves.

No energy reserves, either.

She felt tired. Weak. Shaky.

But hopeful. Soon, she'd get home.

More than anything, she wanted to see her children. Their beautiful faces. She wanted to wrap them in her arms. Kiss their cheeks.

Josh always hated it when she did that. He was too old for such mom-mushiness.

But maybe not this time. Maybe this one time, he'd be glad.

The clouds moved, letting the hot July sun cook the highway's blacktop. The heat soon sapped her energy, and Laura grew weary.

She needed to rest. Needed to find a shady spot, with cool grass where she could lie down for a little while.

But she saw no shade. She was traveling through the agricultural part of the valley, and all she saw was alfalfa fields and cattle pastures.

She had to press on. In a few miles, she'd come to a forested area again.

She stumbled, and collected herself. If she could just get that far.

J acob stepped onto the porch, watching the hail hammer the birdbath in Raven's yard. Lightning flashed and thunder answered.

This was crazy. What was he thinking?

Risking his life for a kid? Not even a relative, just some random kid.

Who apparently hadn't obeyed when Jacob had told him to stay in the yard, where he could see him.

If Jacob ventured out in this storm, where was he going to look?

It would only make sense for Danny to have gone into the house. But sometimes kids don't have as much sense as God gave birds. Jacob took a step off the porch and got nailed by the monster hail.

He backed up onto the covered porch.

Seriously, this was nuts!

He could get killed out there. If not struck by lightning, then beat to death by golf-ball sized hailstones.

Of course, Danny might be getting that treatment right now.

He cussed under his breath, then plunged off the porch and started yelling.

"Danny? Danny!"

The storm was so loud, the kid probably couldn't even hear him if he was ten feet away.

This was ridiculous!

Asinine.

Jacob bent down and looked under the raised porch, hoping to find the kid cowering under there. No such luck.

He lit out for the shed behind the house, ducking into its welcome refuge from the pelting hail.

"Danny, you here?"

Lightning flashed, illuminating the interior through the open door and the windows. An old lawnmower sat in a back corner. Rows of shelves lined the walls. A half-empty bag of garden fertilizer waited on a potting table under the window.

But Danny wasn't here.

Jacob stood, dripping, just inside the open doorway.

He did not want to go back out there. Not for Danny. Not for nobody!

"WHAT DO WE DO NOW?" Willow stared at Candy's pale, rain-soaked face as the wind let up.

"How's her pulse?" Raven asked.

"Same. Real weak."

"We keep going." Raven took a deep breath and blew air into Candy's lungs.

After five seconds, another breath. Then another.

Willow watched Candy's chest rise and fall with Raven's efforts. If only it would rise and fall on its own!

The rain stopped abruptly. Lightning continued, but most of

the strikes were two to four miles distant now. The storm was finally moving away.

Alan and Clark hurried over and knelt beside them.

"We can take over, if you want a break," Alan offered.

"Okay." Raven moved aside. "I'm getting lightheaded."

"She has a pulse, so you don't need to do chest compressions," Willow told him. "Just air."

As Alan began mouth-to-mouth resuscitation, Clark took Candy's limp hand in his own. He placed his other hand on her shoulder and bowed his head. His lips moved in silent prayer.

Willow scurried over to Deborah, who held a sobbing Maria in her arms.

"Is she alright?" Her eyes searched the child for signs of injury.

"Seems to be. At least on the outside." Deborah patted the girl's back gently. "No way to know about internal injuries. And we'll find out soon enough about hearing or vision problems."

Deborah studied Willow.

"What about her mom?"

"I don't know." Willow's eyes began to flood. "We got her pulse established, but it's real weak. And she still isn't breathing."

She was surprised by her tears for Candy. They were unexpected. She brushed them away quickly.

But she'd also been surprised by Candy's immediate, self-sacrificing action to save her daughter's life. Candy had protected Maria from harm, risking her own life in the process. Possibly making the ultimate sacrifice for her daughter.

Willow blinked away fresh tears.

In her own calloused view of Candy, she'd somehow missed some real important character qualities in that woman.

Now, she felt astonished. And ashamed.

THE HAIL and rain let up and moved on, but Danny was nowhere to be found.

Jacob searched everywhere. The house, the yard, the trees, the field behind the house and the forest behind it, then back to Raven's home and across the road to the neighbor's house.

Not a sign, not a trace of the kid. No footprints in the wet earth. Nothing at all.

Maybe Danny had headed for his own home. Maybe he'd done that while Jacob was asleep on the porch. It might have been long before the storm arrived.

Ponderosa was a small town, but Danny was only four years old.

Would he have gotten lost, or could he have found his way?

There was only one way to find out.

As exhausted as he was, Jacob had to walk across town.

Again.

He was too tired for this nonsense. He'd worked all night, spied on the newcomers this morning, hurried over to Marcus's place for some food, then across town the other way to Heidi's to pick Danny up, then back to Raven's house, and maybe had gotten two or three hours of sleep.

Now it was late afternoon. He needed to be resting so he could work tonight.

No rest for the wicked.

The old saying flashed through his mind as he headed out the door.

That was stupid. He wasn't wicked. Here he was, trying to do a good turn for a lost orphan. And he needed his rest!

He began trudging across town to Danny's house. One good thing came from this storm – there was a lot less smoke in the air. Very little smoke was rising from the downtown fire now. On the far hillside, McMansion-ville, there was plenty of smoke, but the rain had at least tamped the fire down some. Once things dried out there, it'd pick back up, though.

Looking south, the big fire out in Willow's Wilderness was still going like mad. Maybe the rain hadn't reached that far. Huge plumes of grey smoke billowed to the stratosphere.

If they had the kind of wind out there that he'd seen here in Ponderosa, that thing might've grown into a monster fire this afternoon. 'Cause it sure didn't get tamped down, by the looks of it. It might've run a mile, or many, in that wind.

When he reached Danny's house, he walked up to the front door, turned the handle and pushed it open.

"Hey! What do you think you're doing?" A gruff voice boomed from the darkened living room.

Jacob froze. Was he at the wrong house?

No. He was at the right place.

"What're you doing here?" He countered in a hostile tone. "This isn't your house!"

As his eyes adjusted to the dim interior, he made out a big guy who launched out of the couch and swaggered toward him.

"It is, now!" The shaved-headed guy got right in Jacob's face. "So get out!"

As much as Jacob was tempted to take a swing at the guy, he decided it wasn't worth it. It wasn't Jacob's home, after all, and the owner was dead.

Still, he should probably knock him out, just on principle. Who did this guy think he was, anyway? Besides, he could take him. The guy was maybe an inch taller, and ten years older than Jacob. His beer belly tugged at his dirty white t-shirt with a faded Corona logo on it.

Jacob's hands clenched and his body tensed – but he took a deep breath, then a step back. He needed information more than he needed a fight right now.

"Look, I don't care if you want to move in. I'm just looking for a kid."

"There's no kids here."

He could smell the guy's breath, and it stank. Like he hadn't brushed his teeth in weeks.

"Well, there was one. Have you seen him?"

"I said, there's no kids here. Get out!" Beer Belly pointed at the door. "Now!"

"I'll leave after I get some of his stuff. You know, out of his bedroom down the hall." Jacob stared the guy down. "He needs some clothes, doesn't he?"

"Not if you don't even know where he is."

"He'll turn up."

Jacob brushed past the guy and headed down the hall to Danny's room. This might be his only chance to gather some of Danny's belongings before this idiot trashed or burned them.

In Danny's bedroom, Jacob looked for a bag or something to pack stuff in. The kid had a backpack, but it was sized for a four-year-old. That wouldn't hold much. Still, he grabbed it and shoved some shoes and kiddo boots into it.

He picked up the bed pillow and stuffed sweaters, jeans and some underwear in the pillowcase.

In the closet, he found a cloth hamper. Leaving the dirty clothes in it, he added a coat, a well-worn stuffed bear, Danny's blue blanket, and some socks.

Beer Belly hadn't followed him into the bedroom, so Jacob pressed his luck and went into the bathroom. Dumping the contents of the garbage can into the bathtub, he pulled the bag from it and began piling stuff inside – toothpaste, soap, a hand towel – then he opened the medicine cabinet.

Treasure trove!

Pain meds, antibiotic ointment, bandages, and some girl

stuff. He didn't have time to sort it out. In one quick sweep, it all landed in his garbage bag.

"Hey!" Beer Belly boomed from the doorway. "You said you were getting stuff for the kid!"

"He needs his toothbrush, doesn't he?" Jacob grabbed it. "You obviously lost yours!"

Firmly gripping the garbage bag, Jacob pushed past the guy, grabbed Danny's backpack, bulging pillowcase and hamper, and strode toward the door, hoping the guy wouldn't take a swing at him.

He'd have a hard time defending himself at the moment. His hands were full.

He made it out the front door with Danny's things, and didn't slow down until he'd gone out the front gate.

Now what?

Heidi's place.

With any luck, Danny had wound up there. If he hadn't, Jacob didn't know where else to look.

He hurried over and knocked on her door.

"I'm in the back yard." Her soft voice floated around the corner of the house.

Jacob left Danny's gear, except for the garbage bag full of bathroom stuff, on her porch. He was hanging onto that for now. He strode around the house and found her in the garden. She stood up as he approached, her denim shorts showing off her long legs.

"That hail just destroyed my vegetables!" She fingered a broken cornstalk. "What am I going to do now?"

"Have you seen Danny?"

She looked at him like he was a dunce.

"You're kidding, right? You lost him?"

"I didn't lose him... he wandered off!"

"Jacob!" She took a step closer, and he almost expected her

to shake a finger under his nose. "He's a little boy! You have to keep an eye on him!"

"Don't insult me! He's not my kid." Jacob stared her down. "I'm doing the best I can. But I can't work all night to feed us, and then stay awake all day to keep him from wandering off."

Her lips softened and she nodded.

"I know. Of course you can't." She laid a gentle hand on his arm. "I'll help look for him. When we find him, maybe you should both move in with me."

Her sapphire eyes drew him in, and he found himself tempted.

"I could watch him while you're working and sleeping. We could take care of each other," she continued, her voice sweet and low. "Like a family."

Her blonde hair looked so soft, he almost reached out and touched it. He had to swallow hard to find his voice.

"Uh – well, uh – we'll see," he stammered. "Right now, I just gotta find him."

She moved beside him and slid her arm into the crook of his elbow, looking up at him with those amazingly blue eyes.

"I'll help you."

WILLOW'S FINGERS searched Candy's wrist.

"Her pulse! I can't find it!"

She reached toward Candy's throat, her fingers shaking as she felt for any sign of a heartbeat.

"Let me check." Raven's voice was calm, her hands quick as she leaned over Candy's body.

The storm had moved on, taking its lightning and thunder and tantalizing but tiny amount of rain with it. Meanwhile, Alan, Willow and Raven had alternated efforts to resuscitate

Candy. While they'd established a weak heartbeat, she'd never taken a breath on her own.

How long had it been? Forty-five minutes? An hour?

The group had gathered around her, praying. Maria, still in Deborah's arms, whimpered and reached toward her mom.

Raven glanced at her. "I can't find it, either."

Alan hung his head.

A sob slipped from Willow's throat. She choked as she tried to speak.

"CPR... we'll start the chest compressions... again."

"I think she's gone, Willow." Alan reached over and put his hand on her shoulder, his sad eyes revealing his grief.

"No!" She brushed his hand away and got into a kneeling position to administer compressions. "Not yet!"

She and Raven did CPR for what seemed like a very long time, but was probably another ten minutes.

Her lips quivered as she blinked back her tears.

No, Candy had to come back. She had to!

Every few minutes, Alan checked for a pulse. And each time, he shook his head.

Finally, Willow admitted what was obvious to everyone else.

Candy was gone.

And Willow covered her face and sobbed inconsolably.

14

L aura finally came out of the agricultural area into a place where the highway ran through a forest. Her injured foot protested every step. Her eyes scanned for a decent place to sit and rest.

She left the highway and entered the woods, grateful for the shade, which dropped the temperature a good ten degrees. It was still hot, but bearable. Perhaps 80 degrees or so.

It had been foolhardy to press on during the afternoon. She knew better, and she'd been smarter earlier in her journey when she'd done most of her traveling during the evening and early morning, or at night.

Walking during the afternoon in July was just plain dumb. Perhaps a lack of food was diminishing her cognitive abilities.

Or maybe it was just her desire to see her children, which seemed to grow stronger with each passing hour and mile.

Whatever it was, she had to be smarter. If she wanted to get home, if she hoped to see her son and daughter, she had to make better decisions.

She sat on an old stump and pulled off her shoes. Her injured foot throbbed.

Maybe it was too soon to see it plainly, but it was getting infected. She could feel it.

The question was, now that she was so close to home, should she press on despite the injury and hope to take care of it when she got there? Or try to beg supplies at the next home she came to, things like soap and antibiotic ointment and real bandages and maybe oral antibiotics?

Who would even have antibiotics at their house?

And who would share any of that stuff with a stranger?

No, she'd have to press on and hope to treat her foot when she arrived at her own home. For now, though, she needed to rest. She moved some sticks out of her way and sank down beneath a big old fir tree.

Nothing moved in the hot afternoon. Not a branch. Not a bird. Her eyes closed on the world.

WILLOW PULLED HERSELF TOGETHER. Raven released her from a hug, and Josh watched her with worried eyes. She reached for her brother and wrapped her arms around his shoulders.

"You okay?" he asked.

"I will be." She sniffled and let him out of her embrace. She took a deep breath and huffed it out, then glanced at Alan and Clark. "How are we going to bury her? The shovels are back at the cabin, and all but one are buried in the trench."

"I can go back and get one," Raven offered.

"No way!" Willow brushed dirt off her knees. "The fire might be there by now. Even if it isn't, that's too dangerous."

"I'm a fast runner," Raven persisted. "I can get there and be back in less than two hours."

"No! What if you get lost? Besides, you can't outrun a forest fire if it's on a tear." She glanced around the group. "Other ideas?"

It might be distasteful, but they had to come up with something.

"We could take her with us," Jaci ventured. "Figure out something along the way?"

"She weighs like 120 pounds," Matt objected. "We already have too much stuff to carry."

"We could sink her in a deep pool in a creek," Josh said. "Just for a day or two, until we can come back. It'd be like refrigeration."

"Ugh, no!" Then, slowly, Willow considered it. They didn't have a lot of options. "Maybe... that might work."

"A bear could find it," Clark said.

"It's so macabre!" Jaci added.

"Desperate times call for desperate measures," Matt quoted. "Look, none of us like this, but what are we gonna do? We can't leave her here, and we can't bury her!"

"Alright!" Willow held up her hand for silence. "Whatever we do, we have to transport her someplace. How can we do that, when we all have as much as we can carry?"

"I can do it." Clark's voice was quiet. "We can divide my load among everyone, and I can carry her."

Willow didn't doubt it. Clark was a big man, and strong. If everyone else took five or ten pounds from his pack, he would be able to carry Candy. At least for a short distance.

"Thank you." She turned to the others. "Let's all take as much as we can from Clark's pack."

They divided his load, then gathered the goats and chickens, and prepared to head out. Willow grabbed the shoe that had blown off Candy's foot.

"She will not need that," Clark said.

"Dignity," Willow answered.

Clark tucked his body, rolled down over Candy, and emerged on his feet with her draped over his shoulders.

"Whoa, what was that?" Matt's eyes were wide.

"Ranger roll," Clark said. "And this is a fireman's carry."

"You'll show us how to do that some time, right?"

"Perhaps. You might need it."

They headed out, cresting a small hill and then dipping into a ravine. Raven caught up with Willow.

"I have a thought."

"Shoot." Willow glanced at her.

"These rocks," she pointed up the ravine at the loose shale. "We could bury Candy here, instead of... well, you know. The creek idea, where we'd have to return soon and move her again."

"Bury her under rocks?"

"You know, like a cairn. My people used to do this."

Willow stopped walking. As the group caught up, she looked at all the loose rock around them. Why not?

"What about bears?" She asked Raven. "They will smell her."

"There will be a lot of rocks. A bunch of big ones."

"Bears can move rocks."

"This is still the best idea. Trust me."

"Okay." Willow shrugged out of her backpack. "We'll do it."

The group gathered around, and Raven explained the plan. They selected a site, and Clark set Candy's body down as carefully as he could between a few large rocks. She was still wearing one shoe.

Willow pulled the matching shoe from her pack and prepared to put it on Candy's foot.

"Wait." Deborah looked at her. "Someone might really need a pair of shoes in the future. It's no disrespect to her."

Willow stopped. That was one of the things that was so difficult now. It was like she straddled two worlds – the civilized one she'd grown up in, and the crazy one she currently inhabited. In that past world, she would be shocked if someone suggested removing shoes before burying a friend. But nowadays, traditional dignity was shoved aside for practical reasons. Shoes were essential and wore out fast. Replacements could not be easily obtained.

Candy's shoes were in good shape. They might fit Deborah, or Jaci, or the teens. They were only a size larger than Willow's own size 8s.

"You're right." She stepped back. Deborah moved forward and removed Candy's other shoe, which she handed to Willow.

Willow shoved the pair in her pack.

She sighed.

Another funeral.

Deborah took Maria on a short walk as the group mounded rocks of all sizes over Candy's body. When the pile was about four feet high, Deborah returned with the girl. She looked around for her mother, and got fussy. Beth offered to play with her, and Maria smiled and reached for the girl's outstretched arms.

"Take Gilligan, and stay close," Deborah said, handing the toddler to her granddaughter.

Willow swallowed hard. Maria would suffer the same loss as she had, losing her mother. Of course, she'd never had the opportunity to meet her dad.

Her dad. Also Willow's dad. That secret ate at her every day. She glanced at her brother. Should she tell Josh that Maria was their half-sister? How would he take it?

It would devastate his memory of their father. But it would give him a new sibling.

She had to tell him. Some day.

But what if she waited too long? What if she was killed or captured before she worked up the nerve to tell him? Then he'd never know.

She glanced at Raven, who was watching her. Maybe reading her mind. She swallowed again.

"Alan, would you – " Tears welled up. She met his hazel eyes, then glanced away without finishing her sentence.

"Of course." He looked at the gathered faces. "Let's pray."

He stretched out one hand toward his wife, and the other to Delia. In moments, everyone had joined hands as they encircled the cairn. He bowed his head and prayed a quiet prayer for peace and comfort, and commending Candy's spirit to the arms of Jesus.

Alan pulled his Bible from his backpack and quickly flipped toward the back of the well-worn book.

"I'll be reading from Second Corinthians, chapter five. Let's start with verses six through eight."

His grey hair matched the color of the wildfire smoke that made the air hazy as the afternoon grew hotter. Alan's eyes scanned the page as he read the passage.

"So we are always confident, knowing that while we are home in the body we are absent from the Lord. For we walk by faith, not by sight. We are confident, yes, well pleased rather to be absent from the body and to be present with the Lord."

He took a long moment to let this sink in before he continued.

"The Apostle Paul is saying that it's better to die and be with the Lord, than to stay alive on this planet. As Christians, we really need to adopt this perspective, especially at this point in history, when we are constantly faced with tribulation and persecution."

Willow looked at her brother. Was he hearing this? As a young teen, maybe falling in love for the first time, could he comprehend and accept this message?

Josh was staring at his toes. Then Matt nudged him, and he

looked up. And saw Willow watching him. He turned his focus to Alan. Maybe he hadn't even been listening.

"If we could truly believe this and embrace it, we could fully celebrate the death of a believer," Alan went on. "Those who have died have the better deal than those of us who are left here. They're in Heaven, with the Lord! We're still here. It's like they've graduated, and we're still in high school. Algebra."

He looked at Josh, who visibly shuddered. Math was never his thing. In spite of her somber mood, Willow felt a smile tug at the corners of her mouth.

"Before he died, my dad told me not to cry for him when he died. He was going to be with the Lord!" Alan swatted a gnat on his wrist, nearly dropping his Bible. "Dad told me I could cry for myself, because I'd miss him when he was gone. But I wasn't to cry for him."

He glanced at his daughter and granddaughters.

"I want you to remember that when I'm gone, too. Same thing goes for us."

Then his eyes turned to the whole group.

"Today, the same thing goes for all of us. Let's shed our tears, not for Candy, but for our loss of her. For the empty spot that she leaves in our group and in our lives. But don't cry for her. She's having the best day of her life!"

His wife nodded and reached for his arm. He tucked her hand into his elbow and gave her a quick smile.

"The passage continues with encouragement and a warning. Verses nine through eleven read: 'Therefore we make it our aim, whether present or absent, to be well pleasing to Him. For we must all appear before the judgment seat of Christ, that each one may receive the things done in the body, according to what he has done, whether good or bad. Knowing, therefore, the terror of the Lord, we persuade men; but we are well known to God, and I also trust are well known in your consciences.'"

Alan closed his Bible.

"Let's let this serve as encouragement to focus on being well pleasing to the Lord. Each of us will stand before Him one day soon. We will be judged for what we have done in this life."

JACOB YAWNED. The sky had darkened into complete night, and the full moon was rising over the mountain range. Stars filled the universe overhead.

He shouldered the farmer's rifle and stepped out along the northern fence line. He wiped his dry, gritty eyes.

Exhausted didn't begin to describe it. His brain felt like mush. His muscles like mud.

He was desperate for sleep. As soon as this shift ended, he'd drag himself back to Raven's house and collapse. He wouldn't get up for anything, not until he'd slept a good ten hours or more.

The end of the world would have to wait.

He blinked and yawned again.

Could he even make it through this shift?

Maybe he could sit at the base of that old cedar. It was a decent vantage point. He could see two thirds of the property from there, once the moon had fully risen.

But if he sat and leaned back against anything, he'd be asleep in moments.

So he walked on past the tree and continued to the property corner.

His thoughts drifted to Danny. The kid had never turned up. He and Heidi had searched for hours, until dusk, and hadn't even turned up a clue.

They'd returned to Raven's neighborhood. He'd knocked on

doors on one side of the road, while Heidi contacted residents on the opposite side. Nobody had seen him.

A few residents refused to come to the door at all. Not too surprising. People were hungry, and they were growing desperate and suspicious. They probably figured anyone knocking on their door must be looking for food. Or trouble.

It wasn't like the houses were actually vacant. He'd heard voices or noises as he approached the door, then total silence inside after he knocked.

Could Danny be in one of those places?

Had something bad happened to him?

Did someone grab the kid right out of his yard while Jacob slept?

The thought hit him like a sucker punch. Regardless of what had actually happened to Danny, it was Jacob's fault. He'd taken the kid under his wing, even if only for a few days, even if grudgingly.

Danny was his responsibility. And he'd failed. Miserably.

He rubbed his eyes.

Sleep deprivation was giving him tunnel vision. He needed to keep his eyes moving, his head turning. He had to keep up his situational awareness.

He pressed on toward the southern boundary, which bordered the road, forcing himself to look around and pay attention.

His eyelids were drooping. He widened his eyes, then blinked repeatedly. His shift had barely begun. How was he going to stay awake?

Turning at the southeast corner, he started along the southern boundary. Trees had been planted, or perhaps left, along this boundary decades ago to form a screen from the road. It gave the farm house privacy, and maybe it cut down the dust.

But from a security standpoint, it was a mixed blessing. Sure, strangers couldn't get an easy glimpse of the farm as they drove past, but it was a great hiding spot for bad guys, too.

These days, no one was driving past at high speeds. People were walking past, and they had plenty of time to snoop as they went. For one, they could peer up the driveway, and for two, they could walk into the trees to scope the place out.

He forced his mush mind to stay alert as he worked his way along the line, finally reaching the southwest corner and turning north.

The farmer hadn't said Jacob had to continuously walk the perimeter of his property all night, but since he was the lone security guard, it only made sense. He didn't have a lookout tower where he could survey the whole place from one location.

Although... he turned and glanced toward the barn. It might be tall enough.

Nah. There weren't enough windows on each side that were high enough for a good vantage point. Too bad, though, because it could make a good observation post with a little remodeling.

He pressed on to the northwest corner. To avoid tripping in the dark, he watched each step. Then reminded himself to look up and around. His exhausted tunnel vision was growing worse.

The cedar grove with that huge cedar loomed ahead.

His eyes watered as he yawned. He was too tired to press on.

Jacob knew he couldn't afford to fall asleep. It was too dangerous. He'd just sit down for a minute and gather his energy.

15

J acob jerked awake. Where was he? His eyes scanned the darkness as he scrambled to his feet.

His hand felt rough bark. His rifle slipped, and he lunged for it, grabbing it before it hit the dirt.

He was at the cedar grove.

How long had he been asleep? The moon was high overhead. Last he remembered, it'd just been coming up. That meant hours, right?

Rubbing his eyes, he looked around. Everything was quiet. What had woken him up?

Whatever it had been, it was a good thing he'd awakened. He'd been sleeping on the job! He wasn't that kind of guy.

Standing at the base of the tree, he gathered his wits. He didn't see or hear anything suspicious, but something felt off.

He remained motionless, letting his senses take in everything they could pick up. The cool breeze on his face. The sound of a dog barking far in the distance. The swaying of the limbs overhead. The smell of dust. And distant wildfire smoke.

His eyes swept the moonlit farm. The house, the barn, the chicken coop, the potato fields... all appeared quiet.

So he was just being jumpy. He yawned and stretched, then shouldered the rifle and stepped out toward the northeast corner.

Now, he had to stay alert. Keep his head turning, his eyes moving. He turned at the property corner and started south, toward the trees along the road.

After he'd covered more than half the distance, he froze.

Did something just move in the trees ahead?

Or had he imagined it?

He was out in the open along the eastern fence. He had no cover here! Gripping the rifle firmly, he broke into a sprint toward the nearest cover, which happened to be the trees where he thought he'd seen something move.

Reaching the trees, he darted among the branches, found a good, big trunk, and eased up to it. Despite the full moon, it was really difficult to make out anything in the trees.

If only he had night vision!

His heart pounded, muddling his hearing, and he took a long, deep breath and held it to slow his heart rate.

It didn't help. He didn't hear a thing.

Until a twig snapped.

His head turned sharply toward the sound. It was close, maybe thirty feet away or less.

Someone was here!

LAURA SHIVERED AS SHE AWOKE. The cold ground sapped the warmth from her body. She sat up and looked around in the dim moonlight.

When she'd fallen asleep, it was mid-afternoon. Now it was the middle of the night. She'd slept a long time.

She was hungry. When was the last time she'd eaten? Too long ago.

If she was going to make it, she had to take care of herself. Needed to find something to eat. But where?

She pulled herself to her feet and was instantly reminded of her injury. The sole of her foot throbbed.

It needed to be cleaned, but that was an exercise in futility, even if she could find pure water again. It'd get dirty as soon as the road dust worked its way through her makeshift cotton bandage.

Well, she'd do the best she could as soon as she could.

For now, she'd start walking. It was a good time to walk. Cool and dark.

She found her way out to the highway and started north, leaning into her walking stick as she stepped on her bad foot.

Ponderosa was so close now! If she were in good health and uninjured, she might be able to get home today!

Realistically, if she made it halfway today in this condition, she'd be doing well. Maybe she could get there tomorrow.

She imagined walking in the front door. Wrapping her children in her arms. Treating her foot. Putting it up on the ottoman as she sank into her favorite rocking chair in the living room.

Maybe it was delusional. Her kids probably wouldn't be there. They had probably, hopefully, fled town after she was detained.

Still, she let imagination run loose. Hugging Willow and Josh. Smelling dinner that Willow had prepared in the kitchen. Pizza – no, maybe roast chicken and new potatoes, with a fabulous side salad from the garden.

And ice cream for dessert! With apple pie!

She chuckled at her crazy wishful thinking.

Okay, maybe more realistically, she'd let herself into a dark, quiet house. She'd call out for the kids and be a little relieved when they didn't answer. Hobbling into the kitchen, maybe she'd find a bottle of water in the warm fridge. She'd drink half and use the other half to clean her foot.

She'd get some ointment from the cabinet in the bathroom, then dress the wound properly, take two aspirin and climb into her own, amazingly comfortable bed.

The following morning, she'd figure out what to do next. Which would, of course, focus on trying to locate her children.

In the distance, a coyote yipped, then howled. A second one chimed in, then a third, and suddenly there was a chorus of coyote voices.

She shivered. What if they weren't coyotes, but wolves?

She had no way to defend herself.

Picking up her pace, she eventually approached an old gas station. The pumps had gone out of business years ago, but the owner had kept the mini mart open. A succession of owners had tried running the place. One had put a coffee shop in the back corner. It had been kind of cute, actually.

Laura remembered taking Willow there on her fourteenth birthday for her very first coffee drink. A mocha milkshake.

After tasting the first sip, Willow's eyes had rolled in amazed delight.

"I can't believe you and Dad never let me have coffee!" She'd stared at Laura like she'd withheld the secret of the universe from her.

"Kids shouldn't drink coffee. It's not good for them," Laura had recited for the umpteenth time.

"You also didn't let me have any sugar until I was three! THREE!" Willow had taken another long, mesmerized sip. "But you let Josh."

"Parents are stricter with their first children, I guess," Laura had answered.

Now, she came to a stop in front of the store. The door hung open. It'd probably been ransacked weeks ago.

Still, what if something had been overlooked?

A box of crackers under a box of paper towels in the back room or something?

Or some hydrogen peroxide and bandages?

She hobbled toward the door. Leaning her walking stick against the wall, she peered inside. It was pitch black in there. And silent.

She shuffled in carefully, trying not to stumble or trip on any debris that might be cluttering the floor. The moon cast an orange light through the front windows and onto the ends of the shelves. Beyond that, it was truly dark.

From what she could make out on the ends of the shelving, everything had been taken already. Someone had left one torn candy wrapper on the bottom shelf, and that was it.

Maybe this was a waste of time.

Worse, maybe it was a dangerous waste of time.

But maybe it wasn't.

Laura retrieved her walking stick and used it like a blind person uses a white cane, sweeping it slowly across her path as she headed for the sales counter. Once there, she ran her hand carefully over the shelves below the countertop. They were dusty and cluttered with books, pens, gum wrappers, and.... Yes! Her fingers closed around a flashlight. She yanked it out and fumbled for the switch.

A feeble incandescent light illuminated the floor, and she was in business. With an incandescent bulb, it must be a really old style flashlight. Maybe decades old!

She'd have to hurry. The batteries were dying.

First, she grabbed a couple of plastic shopping bags.

Shining the light around the mini mart, she saw three aisles of empty shelves. The back corner, where the coffee shop had been a few years ago, now featured a hardware display – but everything was gone except some tape and some rope.

The flashlight dimmed and flickered.

Laura hurried back to the employee-only restroom. It was small and dingy.

But there was still half a roll of toilet paper!

And a bunch of paper towels!

A plastic soap dispenser rested on the stained sink, and there was a tiny bit left in the bottom.

She shoved all these into a plastic bag, then opened the cabinet under the sink. There were cleaning supplies and a dirty old first aid kit.

With trembling hands, she picked it up. It felt light enough to be empty, but it rattled, so there were still some supplies in there. Her light flickered. She tossed the kit into the plastic bag.

She needed batteries for the flashlight before it went out! There weren't any left in the store, that was for sure. Maybe something had been overlooked in the back room?

She hurried as the light continued to dim.

The back room was a disaster. Empty boxes, trash, torn containers – it looked like whoever had ransacked this place had been in a hurry. Nothing was left on the shelves.

She began sifting through the mess on the floor to see if she could find anything of value. Under some garbage in a corner, she found a box labeled "Expired." She grabbed the cardboard and pulled the top open. Inside, she found two cans of spinach, a box of baking soda, and a small jar of mayonnaise. All expired a few months ago.

As disgusting as it sounded, she put those things in her bag, as well. Shining her light around the room again, she noticed a ladder in the opposite corner.

She didn't have any use for a ladder, but she kept looking at it. A pink canvas tote bag was draped over one of the rungs.

That'd be a lot more durable than the plastic shopping bags she'd grabbed up front! She hurried over and picked it up, and found that it wasn't completely empty. There was a half-pack of cigarettes, a lighter, and a metal water bottle inside!

She squealed and hugged the tote.

"Thank you, Lord!" She looked up toward the ceiling and shook the bag.

The flashlight dimmed again. She hurried to put all her gathered supplies, together with the extra plastic bags, in the canvas bag.

This was great! So much more than she'd dared to hope for!

JACOB FROZE. Had it been a person who snapped that twig, or just a deer or something? Most likely it was a deer.

But what if it wasn't?

It was so hard to see anything!

He held his breath and listened. Heard nothing besides the breeze and his own thudding heart.

Then he heard the quiet, distinctive *click* of a rifle safety clicked off.

Instantly, he clicked off his own safety and pressed his body against the trunk of the tree. The sound had come from his left.

He shouldered the rifle and pivoted left, at the ready.

BOOM!

The sound reached his ears as pain sliced his right arm.

The assailant was visible in the moonlight now.

BOOM! BOOM! BOOM!

He got off two shots, as the intruder fired at him a second time.

Jacob's first shot hit just below the collar bone, on the right side. His second shot hit the guy's left chest. Jacob took aim again, but held fire as the man's knees buckled.

He was going down.

And Jacob didn't want him dead. Not yet. He recognized this guy.

And he had questions.

UNCOMFORTABLE IN HER sleeping bag on the hard soil, Willow turned over. The acrid smell of smoke filled her with apprehension. Wind moaned through the pines over her head.

Was the wind blowing that fire toward them?

They needed to find a refuge.

But where could they go to hide from a forest fire? It destroyed everything in its path.

Not only did she need a refuge, she also needed information. How big was the fire? Where was it now? What direction was it moving? And how fast?

She sighed and flipped over again. She had a headache. Maybe from the smoke. Maybe from the worry.

Her thoughts turned to Candy and her funeral.

Several people shared a few stories about Candy, but most had only known her a short while. Willow didn't trust herself to share anything. They'd sung "Amazing Grace" and recited the Lord's Prayer together. Alan had wrapped it up with the 23rd Psalm.

The whole service was maybe thirty minutes long, at most. Then they'd gathered their belongings and their animals, and continued their march north.

Turning to her back, she looked at the moon. The smoke made it an eerie orange color. A lone cloud drifted past.

Her head really hurt. She put her hand on her forehead. Her fingers' coolness felt good to her head, but made her realize how hot her head felt. She kicked a leg out of her sleeping bag. Maybe that would help her whole body cool, and relieve her headache.

She prayed for help and direction, and closed her eyes. If only she could sleep! She was so very tired.

JACOB RAN toward the man as the guy fell. He kicked the intruder's rifle away, and yanked the guy's handgun from his hip holster.

"Where are the others?" he demanded. "How many are there?"

The man, dressed in a black long-sleeved shirt and black pants and boots, only moaned.

"What's your name?" Jacob grabbed the front of the guy's shirt and hoisted him so his back was against a tree, his legs sprawled out in front.

Blood seeped into the guy's shirt from both wounds.

"You don't have long, man! This is your only chance to make things right!"

The intruder moaned, then cursed a long string of profanities.

Well, at least he was still coherent.

Jacob just had to figure out how to get information out of him.

"Look, I know who you are. I followed you to town that night."

The man stared defiantly at him, his dark eyes like pools of sin. But he didn't answer.

"Yeah, that was me." Jacob squatted a couple yards in front of him, his rifle ready. "I chased you clear off the mountain, and trailed you nearly to town."

"Help me!" His voice was strained and desperate.

"You answer my questions, and I'll do what I can. Tell me about your group!"

"We were ex-military and cops," the man wheezed. "We had a fallback hideout."

"All you guys were cops and military? You're supposed to be the good guys!" Jacob didn't believe a word of it.

"Not all. Most." The man reached out a shaky hand. "Help me."

"Where's your fallback hideout? How many are there?"

"It was just me, man! Nobody else showed up!"

"Where?" Jacob demanded.

"You gotta help me!" the man wheezed.

"Tell me where!"

"Up the road. Couple miles." He pointed away from town.

"I'll start helping you, but you keep talking. If you stop talking, you're on your own. Got it?"

The guy nodded.

"What's your name?"

"Brad. Hastings."

"Okay, Hastings, tell me about your group. How many, how you got organized, what the deal was."

Jacob set his rifle down and moved to unbutton the guy's shirt. The first wound was survivable, but the second looked bad. Organs had been hit. Not the heart, but maybe the left lung. And there was a lot of blood.

"At first, it was just a bunch of us getting together for beer and fun, you know? But some of the guys were concerned about war, economic collapse, EMP, you name it. And they were guys who knew stuff – insider, high-level, classified stuff."

The guy coughed, then continued. "So, we all started buying some extra guns and ammo, setting it aside, just in case."

"Not food? Just guns?"

"Yeah. Guns and ammo. We were gun guys. It was fun."

"Go on." Jacob cut strips of Hasting's t-shirt with his knife, and began bandaging the chest wound.

"So, the EMP hit. We all met at our buddy's house, like we'd discussed." Hastings winced.

"You stop talking, I stop helping," Jacob reminded him.

"Uh, we talked about what to do. Decided we had enough guns and guys to go get what we needed, you know?"

"You mean, form a gang of marauders."

"That wasn't the plan. Not at first."

"But that's what you did." Jacob tightened the bandage, and Hastings yelped.

His breathing faltered.

"My lung!" He gasped, then coughed up blood. "I think it's filling up!"

"You guys took captives. You took me captive."

"Mark – our leader – decided we should start a slave trade. It was stupid, man."

"Everything you did was stupid. Especially coming here tonight."

"I was hungry! I haven't eaten in three days!"

"That's the least of your concerns now."

A flashlight shot eerie light through the trees.

"Jacob?" The farmer yelled out. "That you?"

"Over here," Jacob answered.

"I heard shooting!" Chad Litton hustled toward him, training his light on the man in black. "Who's this?"

"Brad Hastings," Jacob said. "He figured he'd help himself to your food and gear."

"Not on this farm!" He played the light over Brad's chest. "Looks like you got him good."

"You hired me to stop thieves. That's what I did."

"You're mighty right about that!"

Brad's face appeared white in the light. He choked, then spat up blood.

"Help me!" He stretched out his hand toward Jacob. "I told you everything!"

"You barely got started." Jacob moved to his side and got the guy's arm around his own shoulders. He glanced toward the farmer. "Help me get this guy up. We can get him to the house together."

"And then what?" The farmer motioned toward his chest wound. "Besides, he won't even make it that far. He's got a collapsed lung. And he's bleeding out."

"We might be able to stop the bleeding. You've got first aid supplies, don't you?"

"I won't waste them on this criminal!" He made no motion to help get Brad on his feet.

"I'm not gonna make it," Brad rasped, then grimaced. He slumped against the tree.

His breath came in ragged gasps. His eyes stared at the tree tops above them.

"I'm scared," he wheezed.

He whispered a curse as his eyelids drooped. A long, rattling exhale escaped his lips. And then he was gone.

"Willow." The voice resonated like the sound of a brass bell.

She shielded her eyes from the brilliant sun with her hand. She squinted. How could it be so bright?

"Huh?" She blinked.

"Arise and depart. The fire will be here soon," the deep voice said.

"What?" She threw off her sleeping bag and scrambled to her feet.

Before her stood a figure, tall as a giant, and bright as lightning.

"Where should we go?"

"Don't you know? To the cave."

The cave? The one they'd found in June when they were running from Marcus and his agents?

"Take extra water, and stay inside until the flames are past."

"Will we be safe there?"

"You will be protected. But you must go."

Willow trembled as she stood, wanting to look at the angel, but not wanting to blind her eyes.

"Now!"

And with that, he was gone, and she was left standing in darkness under a strangely orange moon. But a quick glance to the south told her more than she needed to know. Fire danced down a mountainside not two miles away.

16

"Okay, everybody! Wake up!" Willow turned on her flashlight, shook out her sleeping bag and zipped it up. "Let's go!"

She gently kicked Josh's feet to wake him up.

"C'mon, time to get going!"

It was still dark, but Willow felt surprisingly rested.

Restored, even.

But stunned from yesterday's loss. How could Candy be so alive and vibrant yesterday, and so gone today? It boggled her mind. Didn't seem real.

As her friends began waking up and moving around, Willow rolled up her sleeping bag.

"What's going on?" Jaci rubbed her eyes.

"The fire's coming. Look over there!"

A flaming mountain was hard to miss.

Jaci scrambled to her feet and woke up her daughters. The men began packing gear. Maria nestled in Deborah's arms, where she'd finally fallen asleep after fitfully crying for her mom deep into the night. Deborah pulled away from her without waking her up.

"Good job, Grandma," Willow smiled. "Let's let her sleep as long as she can. We'll be carrying her the rest of the way."

"The rest of the way where?" Raven asked.

"To the cave."

"Oh." Raven paused. "You sure about that? We could get cooked alive in there."

"I am sure. I had a visitor."

"A shiny one?"

Willow smiled. "Yep!"

"The cave it is, then!" Raven laced her boots.

By the time the group was ready to move out, dawn had lightened the sky and Willow put away her flashlight. She glanced at Raven.

"I'm so glad you brought that little solar battery charger! I'm going to need to charge my batteries pretty soon."

"I'm just glad I had it, and the presence of mind to pack it when we left town." Raven got a thoughtful look on her face, but didn't say anything more.

"What?" Willow asked.

"I was just thinking – well, the cave isn't so far from Ponderosa. Maybe we could get some supplies, maybe some news about the EMP or your mom –"

"You're kidding, right? Your brother is searching for you!" Willow shook her head. "No way. Besides, it's a whole day's hike."

"Not for me. Not with my running shoes."

Raven the Runner. The Marathon Maniac. She had a few nicknames. And it was true, it wouldn't take her all day. If she ran alone, she could cover tremendous distances in surprisingly little time.

But no. Even if she eluded Marcus while she was there, she wouldn't be able to bring back many supplies by herself. And if anything happened... if she got lost, or injured, or attacked... no. No way.

"I can't afford to lose you." Willow turned away from her friend and moved out, the group straggling in behind her as the sky lightened into a dirty grey, smoky-smog morning.

She still couldn't believe Candy was gone. Yesterday, she was perfectly fine. Right up until the thunderstorm. Today, she was buried under a pile of rocks. Well, her body was. She herself, the real Candy, was probably dancing in Heaven.

It was surreal. Almost unreal.

Willow wasn't about to let anyone else out of her sight. Who knew what might happen?

Of course, Candy had been in her sight when lightning struck.

It was so crazy. So devastatingly, heartbreakingly, shocking.

She didn't smile at the pun in her thoughts. She just sighed and kept walking.

JACOB STUMBLED toward Marcus's house, too exhausted to think. He was gonna get his food, go home, and fall into the deepest sleep he'd ever known.

The night shift was bad enough for a daytime kind of guy, but going two days on three hours' worth of sleep was nuts. Never again.

He walked up the steps and pounded on the front door. It was early, but Marcus should be awake. If he wasn't, he would be now!

As he lifted his hand to knock again, the door opened and Marcus stood there, shocks of hair standing out at ugly angles from his head.

"Hey." He held the door open. "C'mon in."

Jacob stepped inside. Maybe he should just crash on the couch. He wasn't sure he could walk another mile. That couch looked pretty good.

And he'd slept on it before.

He flopped down.

"Long night?" Marcus asked.

"Two long nights, and a day in between spent searching for that kid. Then I got shot." Jacob closed his eyes.

"I saw that little bandage on your arm, but – wow!" Marcus raked his fingers through his unruly hair. "Who shot you, man?"

"Some guy who wanted to rob the farm. Just a superficial wound." Jacob yawned. "Guess that's why they pay me the big bucks."

"That's it, you're done out there. No sense getting shot for a bowl of oatmeal or a little bag of potatoes."

"It makes sense if you don't have anything else to eat."

"And you said you searched for the kid? Did he turn up?"

"Nope. He ran off in that big storm yesterday. I looked and looked. Nothing."

"You're better off without him. More chow for you." Marcus brought a paper bag with Jacob's food wages into the living room and dropped it on the coffee table. "You sure you want to keep the job?"

"Until something better turns up."

Marcus shook his head. "Anything's better than getting shot."

"Tell me about it." Jacob closed his eyes. "I'm gonna get some shuteye if you don't mind. Too tired to walk home."

Marcus wandered off and Jacob fell into dark, silent bliss.

When he awoke, it was mid-afternoon. He must have slept eight or nine hours.

He yawned, then stretched and sat up.

Still felt exhausted. And groggy.

There was a piece of notebook paper on the coffee table, with his name on it. He picked it up.

"Jacob – stop by the station later. There's something I want you to see."

Huh. He scratched his chin. Maybe the kid had shown up, or somebody had turned him in at the police department or something.

He stood, tucked the note in his pocket, and grabbed his grub bag. He was starving. In the kitchen, he fixed and ate a bowl of oatmeal, then headed out the door.

Hopefully, whatever Marcus planned to show him was a good thing, and not a bad one.

It was a fairly short walk to the police station, but it was hot and Jacob was sweating when he arrived. An officer guarded the entrance to the building.

"What do you need?" The officer glared at him.

"Marcus Laramie asked me to come by."

"He did, did he?"

Jacob nodded. What was up with this guy? Suspicious? Power trip?

"What's your name?"

"Jacob Myers."

"Wait here." The officer stepped inside and let the door lock behind him.

Sheesh, did the P.D. think the town was going to siege the building or something? They were turning the place into a fortress.

Well, the police *had* stolen the food from the grocery store, or confiscated it or whatever. So maybe they were right to worry. People were getting really hungry.

Jacob crossed his arms. The sun, tinted red from the forest fires, still beat mercilessly on his face. It was getting real hot out here in the parking lot.

Finally, the door opened and the officer came out.

"You can go in." He held the door until Jacob stepped through, then let it click closed.

Jacob's eyes adjusted to the dim, unlit interior. There weren't a lot of windows. A lobby was straight ahead of him, so he opened that door and stepped inside.

Marcus was waiting there with a black plastic garbage bag tied closed at the top. He held it out.

"Don't open it here. Take it to Raven's and open it there."

"What?" Jacob accepted the bag. It was more bulky than heavy. "Why so mysterious?"

"You'll see when you open it."

WILLOW STOPPED at the crest of a hill and glanced back to check on her group. She saw a lot of hot, red faces, and was sure hers looked the same. With all the animals and with the older adults in the group, this hike had taken longer than she'd expected. But they were almost there now.

Which was good, because the fire was gaining on them.

There had been a steady southern breeze all afternoon, helping the fire run north faster than it would have on its own. Which was probably pretty fast anyway, given how big that thing had gotten.

Its smoke rose into the stratosphere, choking the sunlight. It was so thick, she could actually look straight at the sun without any discomfort. But she forced herself to avoid that, because it would probably damage her eyes whether she felt it or not.

When she happened to glance at it, though, it was blood red.

The smoke tinted all the sunlight so much that it was like a red filter had fallen on the forest. All the colors looked slightly off.

Willow continued down the hill until she came to a creek. She stopped there and waited for everyone to catch up. Gilligan trotted to the water and began lapping it up.

"Okay, let's fill all our containers. Upstream from Gilligan, of course," Willow said. "This might be our only opportunity for a few days, so fill everything, and let the goats drink as much as they can."

"You don't think we'll have any more water for days?" Jaci asked.

"I don't know how long we'll have to hole up in that cave," Willow answered. "It depends on how long it takes for the fire to reach us, and then how long afterwards until it's safe to leave. Yeah, it could be days."

She began filtering water into her bottle.

"Are there bats in the cave?" Delia asked.

"Uh, no. Well, I don't think so. We didn't notice any last time."

"I saw a YouTube video once where a bat attacked this guy playing guitar at a campground in Oregon. It kept flying up and biting his neck." Delia's eyes were huge. "His friend killed it, but turns out, it had rabies!"

"WHAT?!" Beth screeched.

"Delia! Stop scaring your sister!" Jaci chided.

"It's true. I swear!"

"I don't care if it's true. It's freaking out your little sister, so stop."

Delia rolled her eyes and shrugged. "Fine."

She hid a big smile as she turned away.

"Mom, I'm not going in a cave with bats," Beth said. "I can't!"

"I don't think the cave has bats," Willow repeated. "But if there are any, it'll be a whole lot safer in there with them, then out here with that fire."

Beth took several rapid, deep breaths. She fanned her face with her hand.

Josh stood up from filling a water bottle.

"If there's any bats, I'll take care of them," he said.

"You will?" Beth's big eyes studied him. "You promise?"

"Promise." He gave her a wink.

Willow caught her breath. Her little brother, a 14-year-old flirt! That was something she hadn't seen in him before. She glanced at Jaci, who hadn't seemed to notice.

Gilligan nuzzled her hand with his cold, wet nose.

She shook her head, dried her hand on her jeans, and gathered her group for the final stretch to the cave. She couldn't wait to get there. It had felt cold in there in June, but now its natural coolness would feel wonderful.

She'd had enough of this hot, stinking, smoky air.

JACOB STEPPED out of the police station and into the hot July afternoon, the black garbage bag with its mysterious contents tucked under his arm. He gave a curt nod to the officer guarding the door, then headed for Raven's house.

Funny that he still thought of it as hers. She was never coming back, and he was living there now. Still, it was rightfully hers, and he respected that.

He glanced toward Willow's Wilderness. And stopped dead in his tracks.

That fire up there was huge!

He guessed at least 100,000 acres had gone up in the conflagration. This afternoon, with the heat, had made it so much worse. Everything was bone dry and ready to ignite with the tiniest spark. That fire wasn't shooting little sparks, though – it was throwing blazing pine cones and parts of trees – and likely whole ones, ahead of its path.

Even though he couldn't see that from here, he knew it was happening.

It would destroy everything.

And everyone.

He sucked in his breath.

Maybe Willow and Raven had seen it coming and gotten their group out of the way. If they hadn't....

He shook his head. Surely they'd fled. Right?

Starting down the sidewalk, he nearly tripped on a broken piece of concrete. He caught himself and continued walking.

The plastic bag under his arm was getting slippery from sweat. Maybe he could stop in the shade and take a peek at what was in there.

Marcus had said to open it after Jacob got home.

But why? What difference could it make?

A uniformed officer approached, probably on his way to work. He stopped just as he reached Jacob.

"Where you headed?"

What was this, a communist country? That guy had no business asking Jacob anything. But Jacob wanted to get home more than he wanted to argue with this nitwit.

"Home." Jacob moved to step around the guy, but the officer blocked him.

"What's in the bag?" He pointed at the garbage bag under Jacob's arm.

Okay, that was enough. Jacob straightened his back and squared his shoulders. He stared into the officer's mirrored sunglasses.

"What's it to you?" He said it slowly, dragging out each word.

The officer puffed out his chest.

"There's been thefts around here lately."

"I didn't steal anything."

"So, how about letting me see what you got there?"

"So, how about the Fifth Amendment?" Or maybe it was the Fourth. Jacob ran through them in his mind. Oh, the fifth was about self-incrimination. He meant the Fourth, about search and seizure. But he didn't correct himself. Probably this idiot didn't know the law any better than Jacob did, even though he was tasked with enforcing it.

"If you don't have anything to hide, why not let me take a look." His inflection left the sentence as a statement, rather than a question.

"No." He stared the guy down. "It's none of your business."

The officer's hands flexed. Then he looked past Jacob's shoulder and gave a barely perceptible nod. Someone was approaching behind Jacob.

Jacob took one step back and to the side, pivoting so the officer and the person approaching would both be in his view.

"There a problem here?"

It was Marcus! Thank God! Or lucky stars, or whatever.

"I was asking this man to let me see what's in his bag. Because of the recent thefts," the officer explained.

"No need." Marcus clamped his hand on Jacob's shoulder. "This is Jacob. He's one of the good guys."

"He was pretty hostile."

Liar! Jacob bristled, but kept his mouth shut.

"He works for me." Then Marcus looked at Jacob. "Go on home and get some rest. You'll need it for tonight."

Jacob resisted giving the officer a glare as he brushed past him and continued down the sidewalk.

The police were getting pretty big for their britches these days. And why not? It wasn't like anyone could appeal to a higher authority – the courts were closed. The cops had the guns and all the power.

Ponderosa was forming its own police state.

He hurried home to Raven's, avoiding interacting with anyone else he passed on the street. In a few minutes, he'd find out what exactly was in that oh-so-mysterious black garbage bag.

17

J acob hurried up to Raven's door. He'd never had a key, and never gave it much thought in little Ponderosa. He'd lock the house when he was inside, so he didn't get any bad surprises while he was resting. But when he left, he never bothered locking it.

He had no way to unlock it when he returned. And there wasn't much to steal anyway. The good stuff had been stolen weeks ago.

But now, with things getting so crazy, he should try to change the locks. Getting replacements would be tricky, though. It wasn't like he could run down to the local hardware store and buy stuff.

However, after meeting Beer Belly at Danny's home yesterday, he realized things were changing. People were moving into other folks' places. Some had been displaced, like the rich people who lived up on McMansion Hill, near the cemetery. Their homes had burned down, so they had a real excuse.

Other folks wandered into town from other places, like that family yesterday morning who came down Raven's road.

Beer Belly probably just liked Danny's house better than

whatever rag-tag single-wide he'd lived in previously. Maybe he was moving up in the world.

Jacob paused before he turned the door knob.

What if someone had decided to move into this house?

He'd been gone most of yesterday afternoon, all night, then all day until now. The better part of twenty-four hours, or more.

And when he'd thought there wasn't much to steal, that wasn't totally correct. All *his* stuff was inside. Including his rifle. He'd left it there because he was using the farmer's rifle when he worked guard duty. Well, he wouldn't do that anymore. He'd carry his own rifle to work.

Setting the mysterious black garbage bag on the porch, he reached for his Glock before he reached for the door knob.

The handgun wasn't there.

What?

Had he left it somewhere? His mind raced back across the past day. Had he taken if off when he crashed on Marcus's couch? Left it there? No, he didn't recall anything like that.

He also didn't recall having it at work.

Shoot! He must've been so dog-tired after all those sleepless hours, that he'd simply forgotten to put it on yesterday.

Normally he'd never do that. He'd been so exhausted, he got stupid and careless.

So both his guns were in the house. If they hadn't been stolen in the day that he'd been gone.

WILLOW LED Sassafras onto the rockslide, and toward the entrance of the cave. Josh followed with the other two goats. It was a good thing they had goats instead of horses or cows right now. Sassafras, Myth and Buster easily scampered across the broken rock. Their hooves were built for this. Plus, they loved climbing.

The rest of the group followed, with Raven and Gilligan bringing up the rear of the line.

Smoke clogged Willow's lungs as she inhaled. And now, bits of ash and soot fell from the sky. Into her hair. On her pack. Everywhere.

It was like the volcanic ash that fell last month, only worse. This ash came with smoke and heat and terror.

The fire was getting closer every minute. She could smell it, taste it, hear it.

Maybe she was imagining she heard it. Maybe she was only hearing the wind.

But that was scary enough.

She led Sassafras into the cave. Soon, everyone had entered.

"Okay, guys, this is it. Home sweet home for a few days." She pulled out her flashlight and illuminated the interior so the newcomers could get an idea what it looked like. "Let's get the animals all settled back toward the back wall. Give them a little food and water. Not too much, though."

Who knew how long they might be here? They couldn't afford to run out of water.

Her light blinked out. She needed to charge the batteries.

"Anybody got a working flashlight?"

Matt produced one, and she flicked it on to help with the animal care. Then she turned it off.

"We should conserve batteries as much as we can. Raven has a solar charger, but it won't work very well in all this smoke and ash. It doesn't even work real great on a clear, sunny day."

Willow walked to the front of the cave and stared out.

It was a good vantage point. Below the ledge at the entrance to the cave, a long and wide field of rock scree sprawled down the steep slope. Forest encroached as close as it could to the rock slide on both sides, but the slide was about two hundred feet across, with the cave entrance nearly in the middle. Above the ledge, the slide sprawled from the top of the rocky ridge, where trees refused to grow.

And looking out toward the wildfire, she felt queasy. Smoke plumed and billowed from behind the nearest mountain. She couldn't see the flames yet.

But they were coming.

Jacob slowly turned the door knob and pushed the door open. It creaked as it swung. But otherwise, the house was quiet.

He moved swiftly through the living room, making a beeline for the stairs. He'd left his rifle in Raven's bedroom closet, and he usually left the handgun on the nightstand when he slept. Taking the stairs two at a time, he reached the second floor and rushed into the bedroom.

His Glock was still in its holster where he'd left it by the bed. He vaguely remembered taking it off to get some sleep when Danny was here. When he got up after just a couple hours, he'd been groggy. And stupid. Then he'd dozed off out on the porch, then woke up to find Danny missing, and never thought to come back and get his handgun.

Dropping the black garbage bag, he checked the chamber and magazine, put on the holster and slid the gun into it.

Amazing how much better he felt already.

Walking to the closet, he checked his rifle. All good. He wouldn't be leaving it here anymore. If he left the property, both guns were going with him.

Now, then.....

What was in the mysterious garbage bag?

Jacob picked it up and sat on the edge of the bed. The top of the bag was knotted shut, so he carefully untied it and looked inside.

"Yes!" A grin spread across his face as he pulled out the lumpy gift.

Body armour!

Or, actually, a concealable ballistic vest.

It was black and had "Ponderosa Police" emblazoned in white across the back. Well, that would be hidden under his shirt anyway.

Wow!

No wonder Marcus didn't want him to open it until he got home! This was police property. It looked kind of old, but who cared?

Jacob put it on over his t-shirt and adjusted the hook-and-loop fasteners. It was almost a perfect fit. He admired it in the mirror, then grabbed a button-up shirt and put it on over the vest. Checking again in the mirror, he looked a little bulkier than normal, but it wasn't crazy obvious.

He saw a piece of paper in the bag.

"You didn't get this from me!" It was written in Marcus's jagged handwriting, the same as on the note he'd left on the coffee table, telling Jacob to go to the police station this afternoon.

Jacob smiled, and checked his image in the mirror again, turning so he could see most of the back.

Nice!

He folded the paper, stuck it in his pocket, and folded up the garbage bag, too. He stuck it in another pocket. Never know when you might need a good bag. If nothing else, it could be used as a rain poncho.

He thought of his encounter with the hostile cop on the sidewalk near the police station. What if Marcus hadn't shown up? What if that cop had forced Jacob to reveal what was in the bag?

Or what if Jacob, just to make him leave, had opened the bag and let him look inside?

He swallowed hard.

It would have been bad, real bad. He had stolen police property in his possession. What would've happened to him?

Marcus never would have admitted giving it to him, and Jacob would never rat him out.

These days, who knew what might happen to criminal suspects?

The cops probably didn't want to arrest anyone, because if they put somebody in jail, they'd have to provide food and water to them. And the courts weren't open, so there would be no bail or justice served.

Whatever the case, he sure didn't want to find out personally.

He doubted that the police would continue working much longer, anyway. Eventually, they'd probably decide to divvy up the grocery store food amongst themselves, and just go home. Or maybe they'd form a mob-style protection racket – you pay and we protect you; you'd don't, we won't.

It was just a matter of time until society totally disintegrated, even in tightly-knit Ponderosa.

And he didn't want to be around when that happened.

A CHILL HAD SETTLED into Ponderosa's valley as Laura Archer approached the dark town, her eyes scanning the homes and overgrown vacant lots as she walked. Almost home! Would her children be here? Or had they run, as she'd tried to instruct them via a friend's cell phone from the church in Missoula that fateful day?

Had they taken the mark? The thought chilled her to her

very core, and she rejected it. No. They would never. They'd been instructed carefully on the end times and the mark of the beast from their earliest childhood, and they knew the damnation that came with it. They swore they would die first.

What if it had come to that?

For her, it almost had. What if it had come to that for her daughter and her son?

Tears moistened her eyes, and she blinked fiercely.

She swallowed the lump forming in her throat. If her children had been murdered for their faith, they were rejoicing in Heaven now, with the rank of the martyrs. They might be looking down on her, feeling sorry for her and wishing she would join them soon.

If it had come to that, it was for the best. For their best, anyway.

The grief of losing them might kill her.

The truth was, if they were killed for rejecting the mark, they were in the best possible position. If they'd run to the woods and survived, they were still in a good position. The only devastating outcome would be if she found them here in town, with the mark in their hands. All other options were acceptable.

A dog ran out to bark at her, but he was in a fenced yard. She hurried by, head down and shoulders hunched. The last thing she needed was a confrontation with someone, when she was so close to home. It might be someone who knew her, who knew she'd been detained for not having the mark.

Another dog barked a few blocks down. Other than that, Ponderosa was eerily silent. Had the townsfolk been killing dogs for meat? Or were residents keeping their dogs in their homes to protect their dogs from that fate? Or to protect themselves from intruders?

The wind kicked up, pressing her thin summer dress against her thinner back, and raising goose bumps on her arms. The red moon began a grand rising over the mountains, appearing so close she could reach out and touch it. She stretched her hand out toward it and smiled.

Her road was the next one. The semi-rural neighborhood stretched out along the road, winding through large lots and small farms on the east edge of town.

She sucked in a smoke-filled breath. Almost there now, after weeks of walking. Would she be able to find her children? After all this time?

If they were out in the forest, it was unlikely she'd ever locate them. They'd make a point of getting to some remote location and hunkering down. She could check a few of their favorite haunts, but she doubted she'd find them there. Those places were too near the roads, too easy to access.

Her kids knew they'd have to go deep into the wilderness. She'd taught them well. Which meant she'd likely never find them.

And with those wildfires... no, she would not think about that.

She started up her road, walking past the Wilkersons' house and old Mr. James' place. As she walked by Raven's home, she noticed a light. She stopped. It was in an upstairs window. Not bright like a lamp, but dimmer... perhaps a single candle.

Laura continued on, puzzling about that light as she walked. Was Raven still home? Had she taken the mark, then?

Oh, that would be so sad! Raven was such a promising, dedicated young Christian. She came from a broken home. Her mom had died just after Raven finished high school. But Raven had been faithful in church fellowship and tithing for missionaries, and soon the joy returned to her eyes.

Perhaps Raven had escaped the I.D. chip teams. Her brother was a police officer, pretty high up in the ranks in Ponderosa. Maybe he'd found a way to get her off the hook.

No, that was impossible. He might have been able to protect her for a while, but in the end, it was either chip or death. Or torture.

Laura shuddered.

The moon's beams illuminated her home next. She stopped and just looked at it. Like nearly all the others, it was dark and silent.

A chill ran clear to her bones.

What would she find when she walked inside?

18

Willow sat at the entrance of the cave with Raven and Jaci, watching the approaching forest fire. It had reached the top of the mountain just south of the cave.

And it was coming.

In the darkness, it was harder to see the smoke, but easy to see the flames. A whole line of trees burned like blazing torches along the ridge, with massive flames licking the night air thirty, forty, even fifty feet above the tops of the trees.

Her heart flip-flopped as she took in a shallow breath of smoke.

No one could survive that.

It was a mammoth inferno!

Even from this distance, the fire roared, and she could make out the sound of trees exploding from the heat.

She was tempted to run screaming from the cave, and not stop until she got to town. But she couldn't do that. She might make it, but her group couldn't. They had animals that slowed them down. And some folks over fifty.

Besides, what would she find in town?

Crime, violence, burglaries? Marcus?

She exhaled slowly.

No. They were here now, and they'd have to stay put. As crazy as it seemed, this is where the angel had told her to go.

Besides, God could save her and her band of believers, even through fire. He'd done it for Daniel and his friends. They'd been thrown into a fiery furnace, so hot it killed the men who'd thrown them in there.

And what had happened?

An angel met them in the furnace, and they walked around unscathed until the king ordered them released.

Their hair wasn't scorched, their clothes weren't singed. They didn't even smell of smoke.

Staring at the wildfire, that was hard to believe. Everything reeked of smoke here.

Her skin was hot, but she shivered as she watched the wildfire.

How soon would it get here?

LAURA'S INJURED foot ached as she hobbled up to her front door. Her stomach knotted. What would she find inside?

She steeled her nerves.

It was time to find out.

She gripped the door knob and tried to turn it. It didn't budge. It was locked, and she didn't have a key.

Well, not with her, but she did hide a spare out in the tool shed for those times she or the kids found themselves locked out. Heaving a sigh, she stepped off the porch and walked around to the little shed.

She stepped inside, took two steps to her right, and felt with her fingers around the window frame until she found the slightly protruding nail and the house key hanging on it. Clutching it, she walked out and returned to the front of her house.

Laura climbed the steps and took a deep breath as she slid the key into the lock and turned it. She pushed the door open and took a step forward.

"Hold it right there!" A gruff male voice ordered.

Laura froze.

Someone was in her house!

Besides the dim orange moonlight filtering in the windows, the house was dark. She couldn't see anything. She couldn't see the man who spoke.

Did he have a gun?

Would he shoot her?

"Who are you?" The voice asked. "What are you doing here?"

"I'm L-Laura." Her mouth was dry as rocks. "This is my house."

"No, it's not." He sounded sure of that.

Who *was* this guy?

And how dangerous was he?

Well, he hadn't shot her yet, and he was in *her* house. He was the one who needed to answer some questions!

"I'm the one with a key for the door. That's because it's *my* house!"

She still couldn't see him, although her eyes had adjusted to the dark interior. He must be hiding in the shadows. He said nothing.

If only she had a working flashlight and a gun. She'd drive him out. But she didn't. All she had was her indignation.

"Who are you?" She demanded. "Why are you in my house?"

"It doesn't matter who I am. I'm living here."

"Well, you have to leave. It's my house."

"It's not your house, and I'm not leaving."

This was going nowhere. How could she make him get out? She couldn't even see the weasel, hiding in the shadows like he was. She stepped the rest of the way inside and closed the door behind her.

"I'm not leaving, either. I'm tired, and I'm going to bed."

She was bluffing, but could he tell?

Really, what woman could go to sleep with an unseen stranger in her house? It was so outrageous!

He didn't answer, so she started toward the stairs, feeling her way easily in her familiar home.

"No! Wait!"

"What?" She stopped.

"You can't go up there!"

Did she detect a hint of worry in his voice?

"Of course I can!" She started forward in the dark.

"My wife is up there! And the kid."

"You moved your whole family into my house? Why? What happened to your own house? And who the heck are you?"

"Look, we just needed a place to stay, alright?"

Apparently he wasn't going to shoot her. Maybe he didn't have a gun. Or maybe he wasn't a violent person.

She sighed. Could she kick out a family in the middle of the night? A kid?

What if her own family, her own kids were in this situation? She'd hope they'd be able to spend the night.

"You can stay tonight. But in the morning, you're out of here. Or I'll get the cops to remove you."

JACOB WALKED along the farm's northern boundary, feeling better than he had in days. Since he didn't have a kid to take care of, or a babysitter to pay for overnights, he'd gotten to eat all of yesterday's rations himself. Plus, he'd slept twice yesterday – first when he crashed at Marcus's place for about eight hours, then again after he got back to Raven's and tried out his bullet proof vest.

He'd napped in it actually, and was wearing it now. And he'd probably just keep wearing it all the time.

Things were starting to spiral out of control, even in tiny Ponderosa. At first, the cops had kept things pretty orderly, since they were still working and patrolling. But now, most people had run out of food, or they were very close to it, maybe down to a few old cans and stale croutons in the backs of their pantries.

Since the cops had all the available food except for what people could garden or hunt, they'd eventually be targeted.

Maybe the locals would stage an uprising against the police.

If so, one of two things would happen – there'd be a massive fight with lots of people injured and killed, or the cops would quit working.

Either way, it was bad news.

And it was coming, he could feel it. He could see it in people's faces.

He turned at the property corner and started south along the east fence. The moon appeared red through the haze of the smoke.

Jacob stopped. Up at Willow's Wilderness, he could see the bright orange flames of the massive fire as it crawled down a steep slope. It was probably about four miles from his vantage point. Would that fire make it clear to Ponderosa?

It certainly could, and there was nothing they could do to stop it.

If that thing reached town, the community would be obliterated. Nobody would be worrying about the cops and their confiscated food supplies. They'd be running for their lives.

He reached the southeast corner and walked west along the road, just inside the farm's screen of trees. Nothing moved in the quiet night.

What if it came to that?

What would he do?

The Bethel River was the obvious choice. Now that the country had devolved back to nineteenth century life, rivers probably provided the quickest routes of travel for those who didn't have a horse.

Of course, he didn't own a boat. Could he build a raft?

Probably not one he'd trust in that much current.

Well, if he knew the fire was coming, he just had to go far enough to get out of its path. If he didn't have a boat, he could hike or run perpendicular to the fire's line of travel.

It wasn't likely to come to that. The fire wouldn't likely get this far.

At least, he hoped it wouldn't.

Something made him feel antsy, though. Maybe it was time to move on. Maybe it was time to give notice to the farmer and get out of this town.

But what better place was out there? It was hard to imagine that other towns weren't as bad off, or worse. Plus, here he had a job that paid in food.

And there was one young woman who really wanted him to stay. Heidi had made it pretty clear; she wanted him to settle down with her. And she was beautiful.

The more he thought about it, the harder it was to resist.

LAURA ROLLED OVER, comfortable for the first time in a long time. She opened her eyes. She was in her living room! On her sofa!

Someone was cooking bacon in the kitchen.

What? She sat up quickly, remembering the stranger in her house.

It was amazing she'd been able to sleep at all, but weirdly, she'd gone out like the electricity as soon as she lay her head down. And apparently, slept pretty well.

A petite blonde woman, maybe in her early fifties, came out of the kitchen.

"I'm making breakfast." She offered a shy smile. "Then we'll need to fix up your foot."

She pointed at Laura's bandage. It was grimy.

"I'm looking for my kids," Laura said. "Were there any kids – teenagers – here when you arrived? How long have you been here? And who are you?"

"No one was here when we arrived. Just a few days ago." She ran her fingers through her dishwater blonde hair. "Would you like some breakfast?"

"Who are you?"

"We're just staying for a few days. We got driven out by the big fire."

Laura knew the one she meant. She'd watched its progress the past two days as she'd walked to town. Well, that made it a little harder to throw them out of her home. Maybe.

"Did you lose your house?"

The lady's blue eyes sparkled with tears. She swallowed, then put her hand to her mouth. She took a moment to gather herself before she spoke.

"I think so, but we're not sure. We had to run when it got close."

"I'm sorry." Laura meant it, and she hoped she wasn't getting conned. Time to change the subject.

"What's for breakfast?"

The lady straightened her shoulders and smiled weakly.

"I'm frying baby potatoes and onions with canned bacon."

Laura stood up and extended her hand.

"My name is Laura. And you are?"

"I'm Jeannie." She shook Laura's outstretched hand. "Jeannie Anderson."

19

"Well, Jeannie, let's have some breakfast." Laura hobbled into the kitchen.

This wasn't part of her plan. Her plan was to get home, get rested and clean her wound, and find her kids. Having strangers hanging out in her house was definitely not part of the plan. Would they discover she didn't have the mark, and turn her in?

She glanced at the propane stove, saw her frying pan on it filled with incredibly delicious-looking potatoes and bacon, then sat down at her dining table.

"Sorry I'm not much help," she said. "My foot's giving me a lot of trouble."

It felt worse today. A lot worse. It was certainly infected. If she didn't take proper care of it, it could become life-threatening. Maybe it was already.

"You just rest, and I'll dish you some food," Jeannie said. "You don't need to do a thing."

"Thanks."

Laura couldn't decide whether to be grateful this woman was

providing the first decent meal she'd had in a month, or whether to be annoyed at the invasion of her home. For now, she was both.

Jeannie brought a plate of the mouth-watering concoction to her.

"Aren't you going to eat? And where's your husband?"

Laura hadn't properly met the man from last night's confrontation, but he must be related to Jeannie.

"He's out weeding the raspberry patch. We will eat when he comes in." Jeannie brought her a fork. "Go ahead. Please."

Laura didn't bow her head or close her eyes, but she silently thanked God for the meal.

Then, very rudely, she gobbled it all up like a starving person.

She was so ravenous.

Finally, every last bit was consumed and she set down her fork.

"Thank you. That was good."

Jeannie eyed her with concern.

"Would you like some more?"

"I'd better not. My stomach can't handle any more."

Laura looked at her feet. She'd left her shoes in the living room. Her bandage was blackened by dirt and dried blood. She glanced at Jeannie.

"Do you have any clean water?"

Jeannie nodded. "We brought a Berkey filter with us, and we've also boiled some. Why don't you go in the bathroom, and I'll bring the water and we'll wash your feet in the tub?"

"Sounds good." Laura hobbled in the bathroom and looked in the linen closet. There was only one clean hand towel there. She opened the medicine cabinet, but it was empty. Had the kids taken everything, or had looters?

In any case, there wasn't any antibiotic ointment or anything else to put on her foot.

Wearily, she eased herself onto the side of the tub, swung her feet in, and waited for Jeannie.

Moments later, the short lady arrived with a pitcher of water and a sliver of soap.

As Laura poured the tepid water over her wounded foot, she flinched and nearly dropped the pitcher.

"Here, let me help." Jeannie took the pitcher and the soap and carefully bathed Laura's stinging foot, then inspected it. "Some of the scratches look like they're healing okay, but you've got some deeper cuts that don't look too good."

"I need antibiotics." Laura studied the woman. "Do you have any?"

"Not here. We did have some at home, but...." She let the sentence drop, a faraway look on her face. "Well, maybe it was spared. Our house, I mean."

"I hope it was."

"Thanks." Jeannie looked up with damp blue eyes. "About the antibiotics – maybe your neighbors have some?"

Neighbors? They'd probably turn her in. Laura shivered.

"Are you cold? I can bring you a sweater," Jeannie offered.

"Ah, no – I'm okay. I doubt the neighbors have antibiotics. Most people don't just have that in their homes, you know?"

Jeannie nodded.

Laura's stomach rumbled. That breakfast was probably too much. She might lose it.

"Let's get this bandaged up for now. Figure out the rest later."

"We don't have any normal bandages, but do you mind if I cut up a pillowcase or a sheet?"

"I guess you'll have to." Laura covered her stomach with her hands. "I think I might be sick."

Willow watched the blazing inferno as it crept slowly toward her group's hiding place. The fire had barely moved during the night, as cool temperatures in the forties slowed its progress by chilling its fuel.

At the moment, there was just the slightest breeze.

Unless something changed, like a huge storm front moving in, the temperatures would be in the seventies by mid-morning, and the nineties this afternoon.

She turned and looked around the dim cave where her friends were starting their morning.

"Let's have a prayer and praise meeting," she said.

"A praise meeting?" Beth asked. "What's that?"

"It's when we praise God for His goodness and His protection and love."

"Like worship," Delia informed her sister.

"Do you have a favorite song that we'd all know?" Willow glanced at the younger girl.

"I have lots of favorites!" A big smile revealed her straight white teeth. "How about a hymn, like 'What a Friend We Have in Jesus?'"

Willow nodded. "That's a good one. Let's start with that."

The group gathered in a circle, and Beth led the song in her beautiful soprano. Her sister harmonized in alto, and the rest joined in, making the roof and walls of the cave echo with song.

It was so beautiful, Willow's eyes grew damp.

They sang another song, then a third, and Willow's faith grew stronger with each one, and her heart grew calmer.

God had always been faithful. He always would be.

Why did she find herself doubting that still?

Silently, she confessed her failure, and felt peace flow over her.

After singing Rich Mullin's "Awesome God," she asked Clark to begin the prayer part of the meeting. His strong, clear voice rang though the cavern, petitioning for safety through the coming fire.

Raven's voice followed, in a prayer of thanksgiving and praise for all the Lord had done for them already.

Soon, everyone who wished to pray aloud had done so, and Willow closed the meeting with a final prayer.

She opened her eyes, taking in the sight of her gathered friends, and smiled. In spite of the approaching terror, she felt calm. Recognizing God's involvement in everything made all the difference.

He was there. He cared.

And no matter what happened, it would be good, in the end.

AFTER JACOB GOT OFF WORK, he hiked over to Marcus's place to get his food. He pounded on the door and waited. No response.

He pounded again, and waited again.

Nothing. Could he still be asleep?

He peered in the window. Then he walked around the house, looking in every window.

Marcus wasn't home.

And he hadn't left any note or package out for Jacob.

Did he forget?

Not likely.

What if Marcus had gotten caught, somehow, for taking the ballistic vest that he'd given Jacob? Was he in trouble? Was he in jail?

Oh, man! Hopefully that wasn't it. Maybe Marcus just had something he needed to do early this morning.

And forgot that Jacob was coming over to get his pay grub?

Jacob rubbed his jaw. It was getting decidedly stubbly, since he'd given up shaving after the EMP.

It wasn't like Marcus to forget. Maybe he was in trouble.

Jacob walked back to the street. What now? Should he go home? Maybe swing by the police department and see if Marcus was there?

He probably was. If something big came up, he might have gone to the station. He was one of the higher ups, like second in command or something.

It wasn't far out of the way, and Jacob would feel better knowing the guy was alright. He lit out for the station as the morning grew increasingly warm. Cloudless skies meant another scorching hot day.

Not a problem for him, though, working nights – he'd just nap on the shady porch all afternoon.

As he approached, he saw the same guard as yesterday outside the building.

He gave the officer a nod. In return, he got a scowl and a brief look of recognition.

"Hey, I'm looking for Marcus."

"Captain Laramie isn't around." Mirrored sunglasses masked his eyes.

"I was supposed to meet him at his place this morning, and he's not there."

The guard shrugged. "I can't help you. He's not here."

"You're sure? Maybe he slipped in the back or something?"

"Nope."

Man, this guy was a jerk. "Any idea where I could find him?"

"You can come back after ten."

Talk about totally unhelpful! Jacob's jaw clenched. The guard took a step sideways.

"You should move on."

Jacob relaxed his jaw. But his lips were tight as he said, "No problem. Let him know I stopped by."

The officer didn't reply, but his shoulders were tense as he rested a hand on the butt of his handgun.

Jacob stepped back, then turned to go. The last thing he wanted was a confrontation with the police – especially when he was wearing a ballistic vest that belonged to them.

He returned to the street and started down the sidewalk.

Now what?

Marcus wasn't home, and he wasn't at work. Where else would he be this early?

It wasn't Jacob's problem, except that he was missing breakfast. And the rest of his meals that Marcus owed him.

Although he'd been up all night, he felt more wired than tired. Sleep wouldn't be coming until he was able to relax.

Maybe he should go check on Heidi.

See if she was okay. See if Danny had shown up over there, or if she'd heard anything about him.

Plus, it would be nice to see her. A little feminine attention was always nice, especially from a girl as pretty as Heidi. Who wanted to settle down with a good guy.

Jacob rubbed his neck. He was a good guy, generally speaking. Was he ready to settle down?

The sun heated his shoulders as he walked toward her street.

Maybe he was almost ready to settle down. At 23, he was old enough. He was able to support himself, and maybe a woman.

Kids? Nah, the world was too crazy to bring kids into the picture.

But him and a wife? That might be good.

And Heidi was definitely ready. She'd made that perfectly clear.

He barely knew her. But what he did know, he liked. She was

nice, and caring, and took good care of herself and her looks. And her looks were mighty fine, too.

A smile turned his mouth as he started up her block. She was probably the prettiest girl in town. And she was seriously interested in him.

He should get to know her better.

If things didn't work out in the end, at least the process would be enjoyable. Who wouldn't want to spend time getting to know a gorgeous young lady?

LAURA HAD LOST HER BREAKFAST. It was too much, too soon, for her starving stomach.

"I think we need to start you on something bland, like rice." Jeannie handed her a damp washcloth. "And just tiny amounts at first, until you can handle more."

Laura nodded slowly. She looked at Jeannie.

"You've been very kind. Thank you."

Jeannie smiled a wide, honest smile.

"You haven't kicked us out of your house. So thank you."

"Your husband mentioned a child?"

Jeannie nodded. "He's still sleeping upstairs. Let's get you taken care of, then you can meet everyone."

Laura's eyebrows shot up. "Everyone?"

"Him, and my husband, and we have two friends staying with us."

"So four, altogether." She suddenly felt outnumbered. They could throw her out of her own house. But Jeannie had been kind to her.

"Five. Four adults and a child."

"Right." Laura wiped her mouth.

It was her home, but she wasn't sure whether she was the

guest or the host. Did these people ever plan to leave? If their home was destroyed by the fire, and they'd found her home vacant, maybe they planned to move in permanently.

That wouldn't work. She needed to get well, and she needed privacy. Both to hide the fact that she didn't have the mark, and to begin her search for her children.

20

Jacob's mouth felt like the desert as he walked up the steps to Heidi's door. It wasn't like him to get all nervous about seeing a girl. He was probably just thirsty from his walk in the sun. And maybe Heidi would offer him some lemonade like she had when he'd first met her.

He knocked on her door and straightened his posture.

He heard movement inside, then the living room curtains parted just enough for her to glance out and see him. He flashed a smile. She disappeared.

"Just a minute!" She sounded flustered.

More movement inside, and voices.

She had company. Maybe this had been a bad idea. Maybe he should leave.

But he couldn't, now. She'd seen him already.

What was taking so long?

"I'll be right there!"

He waited another full minute, then turned to go. Before he stepped off the porch, her door swung open. He turned back.

She was dressed in a white tank top with lace on it, blue

denim shorts, and flip flops. Yesterday's eyeliner was smudged around her eyes. And her hair wasn't fixed.

He found his voice.

"Hi."

"Hey," she answered. "What's up?"

"I, uh – just stopped by to check on you. And see if you've heard anything about Danny." He swallowed. "Or if you've seen him."

She shook her head. "I haven't seen him. If I do, I'll bring him over."

"Yeah." He felt like an idiot. She wasn't inviting him in. She had company. "Okay. Thanks."

"Sure."

She didn't want him to stay. He should leave.

"Alright, then. See ya."

Before Jacob could turn around, a man came up behind Heidi and wrapped his arm around her waist. As he stepped out of the shadows, Jacob knew him instantly.

It was Marcus!

Jacob swallowed. He stared at the couple.

"Hey," Marcus said.

"Hey." His tone was too high. He lowered it. "I stopped by your place earlier."

"Yeah, man, I'm sorry. I'll get that to you." Marcus stepped to the side of the door. "Your payment."

"Good." He jerked his chin up. "I'll see you later."

With that, he turned and started down the steps, stumbling a little on the last one.

Heidi and Marcus? What?!

He shook his head. When did that happen? Had it been going on a long time? Or did it just start last night?

Jacob turned at the street and hurried toward Raven's house.

It wasn't like he'd had his heart set on Heidi, but – had she been leading him on? Maybe she took the first available guy, or the first to take her up on her offer. Was she that desperate?

Maybe she was that smart. Grab a man quick, while one was still available as the world crumbled around you.

The sun was getting hot. Jacob stepped up his pace.

He hadn't snapped Heidi up, because he'd still been thinking about it. Marcus jumped right in, apparently.

But would Marcus stay with her? Treat her right?

Or was he just using her?

Jacob shook his head to clear it.

Not his problem! Those two were adults. If they were using each other, it was their problem. Maybe he was lucky to avoid Heidi's clutches, anyway.

Who knew what problems a woman would bring?

He was better off without one.

LAURA SANK ONTO THE SOFA. Jeannie had done a fine job bandaging her foot. It pulsed with heat and pain, but she'd endured worse.

The back door opened, then closed softly. Jeannie's soft voice spoke, but Laura couldn't make out the words. A male voice responded, but again, she couldn't hear what they were saying.

She sat up straighter.

Jeannie entered the living room, followed by a thin man, maybe early fifties, with blue eyes. His short brown hair was being overtaken with grey. He gave her a nod as he slowly approached, then a small smile.

"I'm John. I see you've already met my better half."

"I'm Laura." She didn't offer her hand.

"Sorry about last night. We didn't know this was your place."

She stared at him. "You said the owner had invited you to stay."

"That's true."

"But I'm the owner."

"Is your last name Archer?"

She didn't answer. How did he know? They must have come across some paperwork in the house, since they'd been here a while.

"Do you have a daughter and a son?"

"Yes." Did he know them? Did he know where they were? No, he must have seen pictures of her children, here in the house.

She wanted to ask a million questions, but she didn't want to reveal anything until she was sure she could trust these people.

"We met Willow and Josh, and Raven and the others."

Tears rushed to her eyes, but she blinked them back. Could it be true? She tried to speak, but no words came. Her hand covered her mouth as she stared at them through tears.

Jeannie sat down beside her and put her hand on Laura's shoulder.

"They're okay. They're in the wilderness."

She looked at Jeannie's frank expression and believed her. She couldn't restrain her tears anymore. They burst from her eyes and cascaded onto her cheeks.

Her mouth trembled.

Jeannie held open her arms for a hug, and Laura collapsed onto her shoulder, sobbing.

Her kids! They were okay!

They hadn't taken the mark. Of course they hadn't!

She had to see them. Hug them. Hold them.

Her vision swam as she pulled away from Jeannie, swallowing repeatedly so she could speak.

"Where?"

Jeannie's eyes turned to her husband. John sat down in the chair across from her.

"Right now, we're not sure."

"Oh!" Laura's hand clutched at her heart. "Why?"

"We had to evacuate because of the fire. Willow and Raven offered to let us stay in their homes in town."

"But what about them? The fire?" She stared at them for answers.

"They might have evacuated after us. They would have been keeping an eye on which way the fire was moving."

"Why didn't they come with you?" Laura stood up. Her hands clenched and unclenched. She had to do something.

"They had their own group, and their own cabin."

"What? Willow – a group and a cabin? How?"

"She's a strong young woman," Jeannie said.

"Yes." Laura sat down again. This was too much. So many questions... but where to start?

John leaned forward and fixed her with those clear blue eyes.

"Raven and Willow are afraid to come to town, because Raven's brother Marcus has been after them. To get the mark."

"But you – you don't have it?"

"No." Jeannie shook her head. "The fire threatened our place, and they offered to let us stay here, and we thought it might be safe for a while because no one really knows us. They don't know we don't have the chip. Marcus isn't hunting us."

"He's *hunting* them?"

Oh, dear Lord. She'd shoot him herself, if she saw him. Except she didn't have a gun, because the kids had probably taken them all.

"He was pursuing them," Jeannie said. "Before the EMP."

"In any case, they didn't feel safe coming to town," John added.

"Of course not." Laura took a long breath, then looked at the couple. "You can take me to them?"

"We need to take care of that foot." Jeannie eyed the bandage. "You can't be running around in the woods with an infection."

"I need antibiotics."

"That's not all." John's gaze turned toward the window behind her. "There's the fire."

Panic tightened around Laura's throat.

"They're out there... that fire is enormous. Dear Lord!" She choked the last words through fresh tears. She'd been watching that fire as she walked home, never dreaming her kids might be in its path! "We have to go find them!"

"We can't. Not yet." John gave her a kind but firm look. "You can't."

Laura sank back into the sofa. She hated it, but maybe he was right. She was in no condition to be going to the wilderness – she was injured and starving. But she had to do something.

"I have an idea," she said. "We should go to Raven's house. It's just up the road, not far. Maybe there are some antibiotics there."

"I doubt it," Jeannie said gently. "The kids took everything they could. And looters pretty much cleared out everything else."

"But Raven had some natural stuff – colloidal silver and herbs and whatnot. It's possible looters had no idea what to do with that, and left it there!"

She looked imploringly from John to Jeannie.

"We have to try."

Footsteps sounded on the stairs, and Laura jerked upright.

"It's just our friends." Jeannie gave her a reassuring smile.

A woman in her sixties came into the room, followed by a

guy in his forties. And a darling little black-haired boy with big brown eyes and milky brown skin.

"Laura, I'd like you to meet Julie and Mike," John said.

The child ran toward him for a hug, and John caught him up in his arms. "And this little man is Danny."

AS THE MORNING GREW HOTTER, the fire grew louder and nearer. Willow sat just inside the cave entrance, holding a wet handkerchief over her nose and mouth to keep some of the smoke out of her lungs.

Raven and Josh sat beside her, with Matt right behind them. Clark and Jaci kept their family near the back of the cave, where Alan and Deborah entertained them with stories of their childhood. It was the smart thing to do.

Out here, staring at the approaching fire, was downright terrifying.

The popping, hissing and roaring was so much louder than Willow had imagined it would be. Each hour brought it closer to their hiding place.

Was this even survivable?

Would they cook to death, the cave turning into an oven with the fire's heat?

Or would they suffocate as the fire consumed all available oxygen?

Panic gnawed at her mind. She glanced at her brother and saw pure fear in his eyes. Matt's, too. His breath was quick and shallow, his shoulders tense.

"We can't stay here!" Matt looked at Josh. "It'll kill us. We have to run. Now, while we still can!"

"Nobody's running." Willow got to her feet. "We'll stay, and God will protect us. We have to trust Him."

"He can protect us somewhere else," Matt insisted. "This is suicide!"

"The angel said to come here," she said. "He wouldn't lead us wrong."

"You and your angels are crazy. Nobody sees them except you."

"No one else needs to."

"Would you believe me if I told you an angel told us to leave?"

"Of course not."

"Then why do we all have to believe you?" Matt's eyes were wide, the whites gleaming. "Maybe you make it all up!"

"I don't make it up. Plus, the angel has always been right." She crossed her arms. "And nobody is going anywhere. So calm down."

"You can't make us stay!"

Willow didn't answer, but she stared him down. In fact, she *could* make them stay. And she would, if she had to.

Hopefully, it wouldn't come to that.

"Everyone just chill." Raven rose to her feet. "We need to trust God. Today, more than ever. Let's honor Him with that, okay?"

She put a calm hand on Matt's tense shoulder. His carotid artery visibly pulsed with blood and fear.

Josh finally spoke up. "And let's trust my sister a little, too. She's done pretty well so far."

Willow swallowed hard. She blossomed with pride in her brother. She considered planting a kiss on his cheek, but instead knuckled his noggin.

"Thanks, Josh. But really, everything good has been all God."

~

JACOB REACHED Raven's house and climbed the steps to the front porch. He paused and eyed the swing and the cushions he'd napped on a couple of days ago. It'd be cooler resting here, but the bed upstairs would be more comfortable. And with the window open, maybe he'd get a breeze. A smoky one, from all the wildfires, but still a breeze.

He walked inside and headed upstairs. If he got too hot and woke up, he could always move down to the porch later.

His stomach growled. He hadn't eaten since yesterday, thanks to Marcus.

If Marcus wasn't going to be home when he knew Jacob was going to come over for some food, the least he could have done was leave a bag with his food in it. Well, maybe not – it'd probably be stolen before Jacob got there. But the guy could have left a note or something!

Jerk.

That guy better bring his food over pretty soon.

He unlaced his boots and kicked them off. Then he took off his holster and set it and his handgun on the nightstand beside the bed. Finally, he unstrapped his ballistic vest and let it fall on the floor.

Feeling much cooler already without that heavy, sweaty piece of gear, he dropped on the bed. Moments after his face hit the pillow, his eyes closed as he dropped into silent oblivion.

Some time later, a sound woke him. He rolled over and listened.

Thunk!

Someone was in the house! He snapped upright and reached for his gun.

He heard footsteps downstairs... maybe in the kitchen?

It was probably Marcus, dropping off the food. But how'd he get in?

Doh! Jacob had forgotten to lock the door. He had to get better about that. Someone might get the drop on him.

Jacob's muscles relaxed. He didn't need to go downstairs. Marcus would leave the food in the kitchen. Plus, he was still ticked at Marcus for this morning.

Was it just the failure to pay him, or was it about Heidi?

Jacob curled his lip. Of course it wasn't about Heidi. She didn't matter. He was over her already. He hadn't been all that into her in the first place. Sure, she was cute, but –

Was that a woman's voice he heard downstairs?

Was Heidi here? Had she come over with Marcus?

Now he really didn't want to go downstairs.

Hopefully they'd leave soon, and he could go back to sleep.

21

The man's voice spoke again. It didn't quite sound like Marcus's voice. Then another man answered him!

There were at least two men in the house, plus at least one woman! And Jacob didn't have his ballistic vest on, or even his shoes!

Did he have time to put them on?

He reached for the vest. The moment he heard someone coming up the stairs, he'd prepare to engage. As long as they were downstairs, and didn't know he was up here, the element of surprise was on his side.

He tightened the vest straps and reached for his boots.

A stair creaked.

They were coming up!

Had they heard him? Or maybe they were clearing the building to be sure no one was here?

In any case, he didn't have time for his boots.

He grabbed his rifle, shouldered it, and moved toward the bedroom door. From there, he'd be able to see down the hall and spot anyone the moment they reached the top of the stairs.

Time slowed. His heart drummed and his mouth dried.

Another creak on the stairs.

He leveled his rifle and aimed for the point where the person would emerge into the hall.

He paused his breath.

Any moment now.

A rifle barrel appeared first, then the hands holding it. A black boot stepped on the landing. A dark-haired head, plaid shirt, blue jeans... and a familiar face!

"Freeze!" Jacob commanded.

It was one of John Anderson's guys. One who'd survived the attack at the retreat. Mike somebody. The one in his forties.

Mike froze, then lifted his gaze to Jacob's face.

He tensed.

"Jacob!" He said, far too loudly. "What are you doing here?"

"I'll ask you the same. Looking for me?" He kept his weapon trained on the older guy.

"No. We're looking for antibiotics."

"Put your rifle down."

After a long moment where he appeared to be considering his options, Mike slowly lowered his rifle and set it on the floor.

"Who's with you?"

There were other people in the house, but Jacob hadn't heard anyone else since he'd confronted Mike. They'd gone silent. And Jacob didn't know how many there were.

"John's here," Mike finally admitted.

"I heard a woman," Jacob hissed. "Tell the truth!"

"Jeannie is here, too." Mike's shoulders slumped. "We just need antibiotics, man!"

Mike took a step backward, toward the stairs.

"Freeze! Don't move!"

Mike froze, hands raised. "Don't shoot!"

Jacob didn't have anything against the guy, but he was acting fearful and hostile. What was going through his head?

"Look, I don't want a problem with you guys," Jacob said.

"We don't want a problem, either." Mike's gaze bounced around the hall. "Just let us go. All we want is antibiotics."

"I don't want to keep you. We're all on the same side here."

"Are we?" Mike stared at him. "Why you still pointing that gun at me?"

"'Cause you're acting weird."

"Me?" His voice squeaked. "You're the one who disappeared with the men in black, the night of the fight."

"Is that what you think?" Jacob couldn't believe it.

"It's what I know!"

"You're nuts!"

Mike leapt into the stairwell, disappearing from view but leaving his rifle lying in the hall.

Those crazy nutballs!

They thought Jacob was one of the bad guys! After all he'd done for them.

He'd led them to the black-clad captors' hideout, helped defeat them and free Matt, and then chased one of the bad guys clear to Ponderosa, where Jacob had finally finished him off a couple days ago at the farm.

And they didn't trust him?

Idiots!

How stupid could people be?

WILLOW GAGGED ON THE SMOKE. Winds whipped the fire, which roared like a dozen freight trains, driving terror deep into her soul.

As she stood inside the cave entrance, the super-heated wind ripped at her shirt and plastered her jeans against her legs. It was like facing down a tornado of fire. She stared into its maw,

196196

her eyes burning from heat and smoke, her face stinging from the dry, fiery wind.

Oh Lord, help us!

She shielded her eyes from the blaze with one hand, and raised the other toward the inferno, rebuking it in Jesus' name.

The wildfire filled her lungs with scorching smoke.

It blew full-grown trees out of its path, hurling them like matchsticks toward her. One landed on the rocks below her, not fifty yards from where she stood, its flames licking the rocks, searching for more fuel.

At the leading edge of the fire, rapidly approaching the rockslide and her hideout, trees burst into flames before the blaze.

It felt like her clothing was about to do the same. Or her lungs. The wind nearly knocked her off her feet.

Coughing, she pulled away from the cave entrance.

The heat there was unbearable. The roar, deafening.

At the rear of the cave, Maria wailed as Deborah held the child against her shoulder and patted her back. The goats strained at their tethers, their big eyes crazy with fear.

Gilligan stood near them, and began barking. The chickens cackled and squawked, adding to the cacophony.

Clark wrapped his arms around his daughters, pulling them close.

Alan stood beside him with Jaci and Raven.

"Where are the boys?" Willow's eyes searched the smoky cavern. She couldn't see them anywhere.

"OKAY, GUYS, LET'S TALK," Jacob yelled. "You got it all wrong!"

"I don't think so!" It was John's voice this time, not Mike's. "You took off with the bad guys the night of the fight!"

"I did not take off with them," Jacob hollered. He clenched

his jaw so he wouldn't call John a dirty name. These guys might be crazy, but Jacob didn't want a gunfight with them. He was outnumbered.

"Oh, yeah?" John yelled. "Sure looks that way!"

Stupid idiot! Jacob tucked himself into the doorway of the bedroom, training his rifle down the hallway toward the stairwell.

"You gotta be kidding! I chased one of those guys for miles! Nearly to town!"

There was a moment of silence, then some hushed arguing in the stairwell.

"I finally found him again two days ago!" Jacob yelled. "And finished him off!"

More arguing in the stairwell, but no response to Jacob.

"Besides, I led to you their hideout! To free Matt!" He added.

The hushed voices continued arguing.

"Why didn't you come back?" John finally asked.

"I got a job, man!"

"Working with Marcus!" Mike yelled.

Jacob cocked his head. They knew Marcus? And obviously didn't like him. Well, Marcus was a cop. Nobody liked cops.

"I'm not with the police," Jacob hollered back.

"How do we know?" Mike answered. "Do you have the mark?"

Jacob gritted his teeth. This was getting ridiculous. Maybe he could convince them go away.

"Look, this is going nowhere. I don't have any antibiotics. So why don't you just leave?"

The muffled arguing started up again.

"Jacob? It's me, Jeannie." The soft voice floated up the stairs. "We really need some antibiotics. For a friend."

"Jeannie, I don't have any. Seriously!"

"Can I come up and look? In the bathroom?"

"Of course. If you'll leave after that."

Heated arguing drifted from the stairwell.

Finally, Jeannie's hands appeared.

"Don't shoot! I'm coming up!" Her soft voice trembled a little.

"Jeannie, I won't shoot you," Jacob answered. "This is all a huge misunderstanding. I was on your side, remember?"

"Okay," she said, stepping into the hall, her hands still raised.

"Look, I don't know how you guys decided I was a bad guy. I helped you out!"

"I know you did." Her grandma eyes looked at him kindly. "But when you disappeared – and we found out you were with Marcus –"

"What's your problem with Marcus?"

"He's chasing after everyone without the mark! Especially Raven and Willow!"

Ah... Jacob lowered the barrel of his rifle. Marcus was a cop. He'd been trying to enforce the I.D. law.

Jacob recalled Raven talking about her brother, but he didn't know Marcus had a sister. Marcus had been a friend of Jacob's uncle – Jacob didn't really know the guy that well. Plus, Raven and Marcus didn't have any family resemblance. Raven was a Native. Marcus was a white guy. It didn't make sense.

No sense at all.

Suddenly, someone pounded on the front door.

They had company!

"Josh and Matt found a crevice in the back wall," Jaci said. "They're checking it out."

"That's where Candy and I hid from Marcus a few weeks ago, when he found the cave," Willow said. "It's really narrow in there. But Marcus didn't find us. Or it."

"Maybe it goes somewhere." Raven peered into the blackness of the tiny niche.

"I don't think so." Willow's skin crawled as she remembered the spider webs – and the huge spider that had found her in that tight, dark crevice. She shivered at the thought.

She'd survived that, though, and hopefully she'd survive this, too.

Hunching down by the entrance, she looked in. If the boys had taken flashlights, they must have turned them off. It was pitch black in there.

"Josh?" She called. "Matt?"

Her voice echoed out the solid rock chamber. But no one answered.

"JOSHUA!" She bellowed. "MATTHEW!"

Her words bounced around the rock walls.

"What...what...what?" Josh's voice echoed back.

"Are you okay?" She yelled.

"Yeah...yeah...yeah!"

She heaved a sigh. Crazy kids.

Glancing toward the front of the cave, she saw a fiery tree flying past the entrance. She wiped her brow. It had to be over a hundred degrees here in the cave, where the mountain normally kept the temperature around fifty.

Outside? You'd fry to death in the heat of the fire. Or burst into flames, or something.

They might end up baking to death in here. Or dying of smoke inhalation or oxygen deprivation.

Maybe the boys were better off deep in the crevice. Maybe they all would be.

The rocks would keep them cooler.

But wouldn't there be less oxygen?

Plus, she couldn't bear the thought of those spiders. Just the memory made her skin feel tingly, like they were crawling on her. She brushed her arms with her hands.

Looking back in the crevice, she saw a flash of light. The guys did have a flashlight.

"We found something," Josh yelled.

"What?"

"Another cavern!"

Josh squeezed toward her, then wiggled out the crevice, with Matt right behind him.

"We found another cavern!" Matt announced, with a huge smile directed at Deliah. "There's room for all of us!"

"Is it safe?" Jaci asked.

"Sure," Josh said. "It's about as big as a bedroom. Solid rock floor, with a real high ceiling."

"That sounds excellent," Clark said.

"But can we all get there?" Alan asked. "That passage looks really narrow. We won't get stuck in it?"

"Nah, you can make it," Matt assured him. "It's much cooler, too."

Willow didn't doubt it. Her lungs felt scorched from the heat and smoke filling the cave. They might not survive in this chamber. Maybe they could, in the other one.

If they survived the spiders. She swatted at her jeans.

"You okay?" Raven asked, looking at her funny. "Got ants in your pants?"

"Just felt creepy," she said. "There are spiders in there."

"We knocked all the webs down," Josh assured her.

"Yeah, by accident. We walked through them all," Matt laughed.

A blazing tree crashed against the opening of the cave, sending Maria into hysterics. Deborah turned her away from the sight, bouncing her and patting her back.

It was time for a decision.

"Alright." Willow took a deep breath. "We'll try this."

She looked around the cave, which was now illuminated by the huge tree burning in the entrance.

"The chicken crates won't fit through the crevice. Everybody will have to lead a goat or carry two chickens or something."

"And bring all the water you can, too," Alan said.

Those who had headlamps put them on as the group gathered what they would take into the inner cavern.

"Matt, you lead the way," Willow said when they were all ready. "This is it, people!"

22

W illow ushered everyone into the crevice ahead of her. They'd managed to carry all the chickens, and plenty of water. Finally, it was just her and Raven.

"Well, here we go!" Raven gave her a courageous look, then squeezed into the slot in the rocks, leading Sassafras, with Gilligan right behind them.

It was Willow's turn. She had to go in there. Taking a deep breath, she glanced back toward the front of the cave. The burning tree threw embers onto the cave floor.

She swallowed hard. If there were spiders, surely they had run for cover by now, with the herd of animals and humans pressing through the narrow rock channel. And all the spider webs had been knocked down, too.

At least, she hoped so.

Cringing, she slithered into the crevice, pulling Myth along behind her.

She took a deep breath. The air here was more musty, less smoky. And not as hot.

Ahead, Raven's headlamp flickered on the stone walls, casting eerie, angular shadows.

Willow flicked on her flashlight. Since she hadn't been able to recharge her batteries, the light was very dim.

A huge spider ran across the rock floor in the faint light.

Willow shuddered.

She had to press on. Everyone else had already done this.

She sent a prayer up, recognizing her seemingly silly fright, but asking God to keep those spiders off her anyway. Then she moved forward as quickly as she dared across the uneven rocks in the narrow passage.

Myth braced her feet and balked.

"C'mon, now," Willow urged the goat. "We're almost there. It'll be better, I promise."

It couldn't be as bad as this skinny, spider-infested crevice.

She saw flashlight beams through the opening ahead.

Good! This narrow passage was giving her claustrophobia. She scrambled the final few feet and emerged into the little cavern with the goat rushing over her heels.

The air was noticeably cooler here. Almost chilly, actually.

She shined her weak light around. The floor was slightly uneven rock, but fairly flat, with just a few small stalagmites. She guessed that the cavern was about twelve to fourteen feet long, and about ten feet wide, in a sort of oblong shape.

Looking up, the ceiling was probably twenty feet high, but there were stalactites hanging from it. She flicked off her light to save the remaining batteries.

"This isn't so bad," Deborah said, bouncing Maria in her arms. The child sniffled and looked around the cavern, her big brown eyes taking in everything in the light of flashlights and headlamps.

Willow watched her with the affection of an older sister. She was a beautiful toddler. Maybe someday Willow could tell her how they were related. But she'd have to tell everyone. That'd be tough. She glanced at Josh. How would he take it?

Could he accept that Dad had an affair, if it gained him another sibling?

Someday, she'd have to tell him. It was his right to know, even if the truth hurt. He had two sisters, not just one.

"Let's sing," Raven suggested. "Anybody have a favorite?"

"Good idea," Willow said. The din of the fire outside was just a low roar in here. They could sing over it and drown it out.

"How about, 'How Great Thou Art' – it's one of my favorites," Jaci suggested.

"Great! You lead it," Raven said, looking at her.

Jaci's mellow alto voice rose in reverent praise on the first verse.

"O Lord, my God, when I in awesome wonder
 Consider all the worlds Thy hands have made
 I see the stars, I hear the rolling thunder,
 Thy power throughout the universe displayed!"

THE CAVERN FILLED with triumph as every voice joined in for the chorus, which resounded through the rock chamber like a cathedral:

"Then sings my soul, my Saviour God, to Thee
 How great Thou art, how great Thou art
 Then sings my soul, my Saviour God, to Thee
 How great Thou art, how great Thou art!"

As Jaci led another verse, tears sparked in Willow's eyes, and her throat closed as she considered the words:

. . .

"AND WHEN I THINK, that God, His Son not sparing
Sent Him to die, I scarce can take it in
That on the Cross, my burden gladly bearing
He bled and died to take away my sin."

HER SIN. He did that for *her*. Willow was floored and humbled in light of what the Creator of the universe had gone through for her. She coughed and cleared her throat, and found her voice to join in again as the chorus echoed against the stone walls.

As her group sang another verse, she looked around the cavern. If she died now, if the fire sucked all the oxygen from the cave and from her lungs, she could die happy. And perhaps she would. Perhaps they all would.

～

SOMEONE WAS POUNDING on the front door. Jacob cringed. He had these crazies in the stairwell, so it wasn't like he could just walk down and answer the door.

In fact, it was probably Marcus, bringing over the food that he owed Jacob for the farm guard work. Great timing!

The Andersons thought Marcus was the devil himself.

Jeannie froze in front of him, like a grouse trying to decide whether to run or fly. Hushed arguing ensued in the stairwell. They were obviously trying to decide what to do.

"Look, Jeannie – that's probably Marcus now. He's supposed to bring me food in exchange for guarding a local farm." He spoke in hushed tones, trying to calm her. "I need to go down there, or he'll get suspicious and come inside."

Jeannie turned back to the stairwell. "Did you guys hear what Jacob said?"

"Yeah," John's voice responded quietly. "We heard. What if it's a trap?"

"I didn't have any time to set a trap!" Jacob's jaw muscles tightened. "You guys just showed up here!"

"He's right," Jeannie whispered.

Pounding sounded again downstairs.

"Now or never, guys," Jacob urged.

"Fine!" John poked his head into the hallway. "C'mon down!"

Jacob hurried past Jeannie and brushed past John and Mike as he went down the stairs. If it was Marcus, what would he say?

He moved toward the front door. He had to decide, and fast. Marcus was peering into the living room window.

Jacob opened the door but didn't invite Marcus in.

"You bring my grub?" he asked.

Marcus held up a paper bag. "Thought I heard voices. You got company?"

"Couple of friends." Jacob reached for the bag.

"What took you so long to come to the door?"

"I was upstairs."

Marcus looked past him, into the house. Jacob planted himself in the doorway.

"Girlfriend?"

"Not your business. What's the deal with you and Heidi?"

Marcus grinned and took off his sunglasses.

"You had your chance. She told me." He poked Jacob in the chest. "You blew that, man."

"Whatever." Jacob clutched the bag and began closing the door. "I'll see you around."

"Well, hold on now." Marcus shoved his foot against the base of the door so it couldn't close. "You said you have friends over.

Aren't you going to invite me in? I'm thirsty, and it's dang hot out here."

"Was that a BAT?" Delia screeched. "Turn your light back on!"

"WHAT?" Beth clawed at her dad. He pulled her against his chest.

"You will be fine. Calm down," his accented voice soothed.

"I'm not fine!" Delia shrieked. "Somebody shine a light up there!"

"Be quiet!" Raven snapped. "Don't wake them up. Turn off the lights!"

"No! Don't turn them off! We won't be able to see them!"

"You don't want to wake them up!" Raven hissed. "Shhhh!"

Willow planted herself in front of the entrance to the passageway. If their singing hadn't disturbed the bats, maybe their lights and voices now wouldn't, either. She shuddered.

Bats carried rabies. And Montana bats had a high rabies rate – she couldn't remember what it was, exactly, but she knew that ninety percent of rabies cases in her state were attributed to bats and skunks. And in her county, it was mostly bats.

Rabies was a horrible way to die. It was hard to imagine a more wretched way to go.

Back when things were normal, folks who were bit by rabid animals could get a series of extremely painful injections to prevent rabies from taking hold. But now, there was none of that. You get bit by a rabid bat, you get rabies and die a terrible death.

Still, they couldn't afford to freak out. If anyone left the cave, the fire would kill them within minutes.

They had to stay here. With the bats.

"There's BATS in here," Delia's hushed voice was filled with panic. "I have to get out!"

She rushed toward the entrance, but Willow blocked it.

"Nobody is going anywhere," she hissed.

Delia grabbed Willow's arm and tried to pull her away.

"Let me out!"

Willow shoved her back.

"GO. SIT. DOWN."

Delia sobbed and ran to her father, who pulled her close.

Willow smelled smoke filtering through the passageway. Outside, the fire still roared. Possibly even louder than before. It was right on top of them now.

"I can't breathe!" Matt lunged for the entrance. "I gotta get out!"

"NO!" She blocked him, but he was bigger than she was. If it came to push and shove, he would physically overcome her. "Nobody is going anywhere!"

Willow pulled out her Smith & Wesson M&P and racked the slide to make her point.

Would she shoot someone if they attempted to run from the cavern?

Maybe.

It'd be difficult to deal with a gunshot wound, but it would be impossible to save a person who panicked and burned to death.

JACOB'S MIND RACED. To protect the Andersons, he needed to send Marcus away. But the guy wasn't leaving. It was like he sensed something was up. And with all those years of being a cop, he probably *did* have a good sense about that.

Besides, Jacob didn't owe the Andersons anything. He'd helped them out, and look how they treated him now!

Still, they weren't bad people. Just confused.

"Well? Can I come in?" Marcus demanded. He peered around Jacob's shoulder. "Where are your friends, anyway?"

"Upstairs."

"Doing what?" Marcus stared him down. "This is my sister's house. I'm letting you stay here. If something's going on, you better tell me right now."

"Okay, look," Jacob stalled. Think, think, think! "Here's the thing... one of them's a little sick, alright?"

"So why're they here?"

"Well, they were hoping for antibiotics."

"What kind of sick are they?"

"Just a little sick." Jacob planted his hand on the doorframe. "Look, they aren't hurting anything. I just don't want you to come in and catch whatever it is."

"You should get them out of here."

"I will."

"And cover up that vest," Marcus snapped. "Before someone sees you wearing police gear! Put a shirt over it!"

Jacob glanced down. In his haste when he woke up and heard noises in the house, he'd put on the ballistic vest, but didn't have time to put his button-up shirt over it.

"I'll do that. Sorry." He gave his voice his most conciliatory tone. If only Marcus would leave!

"If you can't be responsible, I'll take it back." Marcus glared at him.

Jacob nodded but didn't reply.

"And get those sick people out of Raven's house. ASAP!"

"I will, trust me."

Marcus snorted, then turned to go. Jacob's lungs relaxed, expelling a long breath. Finally!

But he still had the problem of the Andersons in his house. With guns. And they were hostile.

23

J acob closed the door and hoped he'd done the right thing. Marcus was walking away, and who knew what the Andersons were up to now. He looked toward the stairwell. There was no sound or motion up there. What were they doing?

His heart thumped.

He swallowed what felt like a marble in his throat.

"John? Jeannie?"

"Is he gone?" Jeannie called softly.

Jacob peered out the window. Marcus had reached the road and kept going.

"Yeah. Gone." He looked back to the stairs. "You guys can come out now."

John appeared first, tucking his handgun into his holster.

"Thanks, Jacob. We heard everything you said."

"Yeah." Jacob stared at the guy. "Well, I guess you can go now."

"We will. But first, I want to clear up some stuff. It seems we misjudged you."

Jacob coughed. "Misjudged?"

John nodded as Mike came down and stood beside him.

"Sorry, Jacob," Mike said. "But if you'd seen things from our perspective – "

"You never once considered the good I'd done for you and your friends?" Jacob glowered. "I was in two gunfights for you guys! Two!"

"Yeah, but you disappeared, twice! How could we know what you were up to? Whose side you were on?" Mike's voice raised in pitch, and John put a hand on his arm.

"I'm sorry, Jacob." John's apology sounded sincere. "We jumped to the wrong conclusions."

"No kidding!" Jacob's lip curled. "You guys should just leave. I don't have any antibiotics."

"Is it okay if I finish looking in the bathroom upstairs before we go?" Jeannie asked. "We have a friend in desperate straits."

"Fine." He couldn't deny the sweet woman's plea. She reminded him too much of his own mother. "Who's the friend, anyway?"

SITTING in front of the passageway, Willow's chest felt tight. She tried to draw in a deep breath, but just didn't feel like she was getting enough air. Maybe the fire was pulling the oxygen out of the cave.

Beside her, Raven still had her headlamp on, and Willow could see Maria in the light. The child had fallen asleep in Deborah's arms, while the woman sat with her back against the rock wall. They both looked peaceful.

The goats had settled down. So had the chickens. Apparently they thought it was night, so they huddled in a corner, heads tucked under their wings. But one of them toppled over and fell down. It didn't get up.

Alarmed, Willow stared at it. She tugged on Raven's arm and pointed it out.

"I know," Raven whispered.

Had the hen passed out for lack of oxygen? Had she died?

Fear gripped Willow's throat. She opened her mouth and sucked in air. Still, she couldn't satisfy her lungs. It was like she was only taking shallow breaths, when she needed gulps of air. But she actually was taking deep breaths, they just weren't providing relief.

"I can't breathe," she whispered to Raven. "I can't get enough oxygen!"

"Same here. I'm lightheaded."

"I have a bad headache." Willow turned her head so her face was in the crevice. It reeked of smoke. She tried to fill her lungs anyway. They wouldn't relax the way they were supposed to when she took a deep breath.

She glanced back at the group in the cavern. Several had settled down for naps. That was probably the best thing to do.

Gilligan sat next to Raven, gave her a little lick on her hand, and curled up on the floor.

"I don't know if we're going to make it," Raven whispered, patting the dog.

"If I die –"

"Don't." Raven grabbed her arm. "Let's not say that."

"Make sure no one leaves this cavern until it's safe." She stared at her friend. "I trust you. Take care of my brother."

Her eyes moved to the cute toddler across from them. "And Maria."

"You're going to be fine," Raven whispered back. "Trust Jesus."

Willow nodded. She would try.

She scooted far enough from the passageway to lean her head back against the rock wall. Even sitting, she began to feel dizzy. Her lungs felt so constricted.

How long would it be before she passed out?

She couldn't tell whether her friends were sleeping, or if they'd passed out. Or died? No.

She linked her arm through Raven's.

"The 23rd Psalm," Willow whispered. "Say it with me."

Raven leaned against her shoulder.

"The Lord is my shepherd," Willow began. "I shall not want."

Together, they continued.

"He makes me to lie down in green pastures;

He leads me beside the still waters.

He restores my soul;

He leads me in the paths of righteousness

For His name's sake.

Yea, though I walk through the valley of the shadow of death,

I will fear no evil;

For You are with me...."

At this point, Willow noticed that Raven's whisper had dropped out, and she was speaking alone. Raven leaned heavily against her shoulder, then slumped into Willow's lap, her head-lamp illuminating Willow's dusty boots.

Willow's eyes flooded.

"Raven! Raven!" She sobbed, shaking her friend's shoulder. There was no response.

Willow's shaking fingers flew to Raven's wrist, where she found a weak pulse. Her chest rose, then fell. She was still breathing. Still alive.

Willow clutched her friend close to her and rocked, sobbing quietly.

"Stay with me! Stay with me!"

As Jeannie went upstairs to look for antibiotics, Jacob spoke to John and Mike.

"Your friend who needs the antibiotics – who is it?" He hoped it wasn't Willow or Raven.

"It's someone you haven't met yet," John said. "Her name is Laura."

"Is she in your group?"

"Not exactly." He paused, studying Jacob for a moment. "She's Willow and Josh's mom."

"What? I thought she was dead – or captured!" Jacob was sure Willow had told him that. That's why the teenagers were on their own in the wilderness.

"She escaped."

"Willow and Josh are gonna be pretty happy!"

"She's in bad shape. That's why we really need some antibiotics."

"How bad?" Jacob asked. "Is she dying or something?"

"Pretty bad. She's starving, too, so she doesn't have any reserves to fuel her recovery if she can beat the infection."

"Oh, man." Jacob looked at the carpet. "I'm sorry I don't have antibiotics. I'd give them to her if I did."

Jeannie came down the stairs carrying a dark brown bottle.

"I found this under the sink in the bathroom," she said, holding it up. "It says 'Colloidal Silver' on this handwritten label, but I don't know what strength it is, or how old or anything."

"It's worth a shot," John said. "I don't think it can hurt."

He turned to Jacob.

"I'm really sorry for all the trouble. Would you have any interest in joining us when we return to the mountain?"

Jacob shook his head.

"I don't think so. I've got a job here, and... I'm waiting for someone."

"A family member?" John asked.

"A woman?" Mike wondered, a hint of a smile on his tanned face.

"A kid, actually. He just – well, he disappeared. I keep thinking he might show up." Jacob rolled his shoulders. "I'm responsible for him. Think I should wait a while."

John exchanged a glance with his wife.

"How old is this kid?"

"Young. Four years old." Jacob rubbed his chin.

"What's his name?" Jeannie asked softly.

"Danny. You haven't seen him, have you?"

Willow turned off Raven's headlamp to save the batteries. It didn't look like anyone in the cavern was awake anymore. Perhaps they'd all passed out. Matt's flashlight was still turned on, illuminating the far wall.

Maybe she should go back through the passage and see if the fire had moved past. Maybe it was safe to get out of the cavern and find fresh air.

She leaned over, sticking her face into the passageway, and took a deep breath.

Smoke! And heavy. Her lungs seized.

The fire roared.

It was still out there, waiting to kill them.

But she could go take a look, anyway. And maybe, maybe get some air. Her chest felt so tight!

Gently, she removed Raven's headlamp and put it on her

own head, then slid Raven off her lap, leaning her over onto Gilligan.

She pushed up to her feet.

A wave of dizziness swept over her. She clutched at the rock wall.

Everything spun out of control. She bent her knees and sank to the cavern floor before she fell down.

Her hands felt the cool rock floor. Her lungs begged for air. Her head throbbed.

She gasped like a fish pulled from the water.

Was this what it felt like to die?

"Oh, Lord..."

Mercifully, darkness closed around her as her body relaxed and her mind silenced.

"DANNY IS AT OUR HOUSE, Jacob. Or Willow's house, I mean," Jeannie said. "He arrived the day of the big thunderstorm."

"That's when he disappeared! During the storm!" Relief flooded Jacob, more than he'd expected. He'd almost given up on seeing the kid alive again.

"We think he had been under a tree that got hit by lightning," John added. "He didn't speak for a day or two."

"But he's okay?" Jacob grinned. "You know his name. He must have told you!"

"His hearing seems a little off," Jeannie said. "Not too shocking if he was that near a lightning strike – no pun intended."

"But otherwise?"

"Otherwise, he seems like a perfectly normal boy." John gave him a quizzical look. "Is he related to you?"

"No. He was orphaned during the big earthquake. His mom was killed then. And I was told his dad had abandoned them several years ago."

"So you took him in?" Jeannie asked.

"Yeah – I was the one who found them, and no one else volunteered. It's kind of hard to find enough to eat, much less feed an extra person, you know?"

"Of course." Jeannie glanced at her husband, then back at Jacob. "So now what?"

Jacob didn't know what she meant. "Now what?"

"Do you want him back?" She asked. "Or can we keep him?"

The thought that they would voluntarily take Danny surprised Jacob. Before the craziness, sure – but people were starving now. Nobody wanted an extra kid.

On the one hand, he was happy to be relieved of the responsibility. But on the other hand, he had a job that provided food for both of them, and who knew if the Andersons could provide for the kid. It was one thing when they had that cushy retreat in the mountains, all stocked with food. But if that place had burned – if their food was gone – they wouldn't be able to survive themselves, much less feed an extra person.

"We'll need to think about that," Jacob finally said.

"And pray about it," John added.

Jeannie's face fell, but she took her husband's hand.

"You're right." She looked back at Jacob. "I'll take this antibiotic back to Laura, if that's okay. And you can come over when you're ready to talk about Danny."

"Sounds good to me." He walked to the door, then checked out the window to make sure Marcus hadn't doubled back to spy on him.

Not seeing anyone, he opened the door and they filed outside.

"How soon do you plan to return home?" Jacob asked.

John eyed the mountains.

"Soon, I think. I believe the fire has moved past our neighborhood, and things should be about done burning in that area."

24

"I think she's dead!" Matt's voice echoed distantly.

"No," Willow whispered. "I'm not."

Darkness and cold. That's all she could register. She shivered and blinked. Then her head hurt. And she was so thirsty.

"Where am I?"

Her back ached, then her neck. She scrunched up her shoulders.

"In the cavern, remember?"

That was Josh's voice.

"Water." Her throat was so dry. "Aspirin."

Someone grabbed her arms and pulled. She instinctively scrambled to get her feet under her.

"We gotta get you out of here." A strange light flashed across Matt's face, inches from hers. She slumped into his arms.

"But you gotta walk. We can't drag you through that passageway."

Willow blinked and ordered her legs to support her weight.

She took a deep breath.

Smoky, but not as bad as before.

She steadied herself, clinging to Matt's shoulders.

"Water?" She asked.

"You can get a drink as soon as you get out to the main cave," Matt said. "Can you stand up on your own?"

"Sure."

But it wasn't as easy as that. Her knees buckled, and she grabbed onto Matt again.

"Almost."

"C'mon, Willow." It was Josh, behind her. "You gotta stand up!"

She planted her feet and forced her muscles to cooperate, balancing her unsteadily.

"Okay." She kept a hand on Matt's shoulders. "I'm good."

"Yeah, you look it." Matt cocked his head. "You gotta walk through that passage on your own two feet."

She didn't see anyone else in the cavern.

"Where is everybody?"

"They're out. You're the last one."

"Good." She took a deep breath, and let go of Matt. "Let's go."

"I'll go first, then you, then Josh," Matt said. "Just in case."

"Fine." She reached for the rock wall. "Lead on."

Matt entered the passage, his flashlight picking the way through the narrow crevice. Willow shuffled in behind him, swaying a little. Josh kept one hand on her back as she picked her way across the uneven rock floor.

The passage seemed to go on forever. Willow swallowed. She didn't remember it being this long on the way in.

Had they made a wrong turn somewhere?

Were they lost in the belly of the mountain?

With monstrous spiders and bats.

"Hold on." Willow stopped, her head spinning. She braced one hand against the rock wall.

"Are you okay?" Josh asked.

"Lightheaded." She took a long breath. "Are we lost?"

"No," Matt answered. "Almost there."

"Okay." She steadied herself. "I'm ready."

They shuffled forward again, and moments later, she could see daylight ahead. Oh, thank God! She had survived and would see the sun and breathe clean air!

She stumbled out into the main cave right behind Matt. Raven waited there, and pulled her into a hug.

"We were worried about you, girl! We couldn't wake you up!"

"I'm okay. Water?"

Raven handed her a water bottle. "Drink up!"

Willow took deep gulps as she glanced around the cave. The tree across the front had nearly burned itself out. Most of the group had gathered near the entrance, and they were looking outside.

"How long?" Willow asked.

"We spent the night in there," Raven said. "Most of us were passed out, though."

"Everyone's okay?"

"We lost one chicken. The first one that fell over, that you noticed."

"The canary in the coal mine." Willow finished off the water and handled the bottle back to Raven.

"Something like that."

"It's a miracle we all made it."

"Yes. It is." Raven took one of Willow's arms, and Josh took the other. "You gotta see this."

Together, the three moved toward the cave's entrance.

Alan and Deborah turned and gave her somber smiles as she approached.

"It's not pretty," Deborah warned, moving back so Willow could walk forward.

As she stepped into the smoky sunlight, Willow gasped.

Below the cave, dozens of trees had been hurled on to the granite rockslide, where they'd burned up. On both sides of the rockslide, the forest was blackened by the beastly fire that had consumed every tree and bush.

Nothing had escaped its furry.

Hot ash and embers smoldered on the forest floor. The blackened trunks of trees that had remained upright still smoked.

"Whoa." Willow clutched Raven's arm to steady herself as she surveyed the ruined landscape.

And she'd thought the grey landscape from the volcanic ash had been bad.

At least it had let the forest live.

But not this.

The smoke was heavy and acrid. Willow choked, then covered her mouth with her handkerchief.

"Seen enough?" Raven asked.

Willow nodded, and they turned around, crossing to the back wall of the cave where bedding had been spread out. The goats were tethered to some rocks off to the side. Gilligan guarded the chickens near them.

"How much water is left?" Willow sank onto her sleeping bag.

"Just a few gallons. We'll run out tonight."

"Okay. We'll stay here until thirst drives us out. It's too hot to walk out there now." She lay her head down on her mom's sweater. She couldn't smell Mom's fragrance anymore. Everything just smelled like smoke.

SITTING ON THE SOFA, Laura looked at the bottle of colloidal silver that Jeannie handed her. It was obviously homemade, which wasn't necessarily bad, but whoever had labeled it didn't write how concentrated it was. If it was heavily concentrated, it was best for external use. If it was more diluted, it was prepared for internal use.

Not knowing, she wasn't sure whether to drink it, or pour it on her foot.

She twisted off the lid and sniffed the solution.

It was impossible to tell. She glanced at Jeannie.

"Would you mind bringing me a small glass?"

"Sure." Jeannie went into the kitchen and returned, handing her a drinking glass.

Laura poured perhaps three tablespoons into the glass, and lifted it to her lips. She took a small sip.

Oh, it was strong! Metallic taste flooded her tongue. She swallowed quickly, but not fast enough. The disgusting flavor of metal clung to her lips and teeth.

Grimacing, she rinsed her mouth with a gulp of straight water, swishing it around and swallowing quickly. A second gulp got rid of the worst of it.

"Are you alright?" Jeannie asked. "Can I bring you something else?"

Laura shook her head.

"It's okay. It's really strong." She pulled the bandage away from her foot. "That's good, because I can treat my foot topically with that, and dilute some to drink as well."

Jeannie looked skeptical.

"Does that stuff really work?"

"Usually." Laura poured some of the solution on her foot, catching the excess with the bandage, which she re-wrapped against the wound. "Anyway, I don't have any other options, do I?"

"Not too many, I'm afraid. Want me to pray for you?"

"Absolutely, yes!" Laura smiled at her new friend.

Jeannie sat beside her on the couch and put her hand on her shoulder. She prayed for healing and peace and rest, and that Laura and her children would be reunited. She prayed that the kids would be safe in the wilderness.

Laura's eyes were wet as Jeannie finished.

She smiled sadly and hugged the little woman.

"Thank you," Laura breathed.

When she pulled away, she saw that Jeannie's eyes had tears, too. The older lady gave her a sure smile.

"He will answer. You'll see."

"I know He will." Laura leaned back into the cushions. "I just hope it's real soon."

John came in the back door with Danny.

"Mike and Julie are hanging out in the barn to make sure nobody wanders off with our animals." He took off his hat and looked at Laura. "How are you doing?"

"On the road to recovery." She sighed. "Still a little weak, I guess."

"Julie made some plain rice. That might be best for your stomach, until you're able to keep down real food."

"Perfect."

He sat in the green chair across from the sofa and studied her.

"I've been thinking about how to get you up to the wilderness. We want to go as soon as possible, but you can't walk until that heals."

He eyed the bandage on her foot.

"I'm afraid it'll be a while." She stared at the offending foot. "A few days, at least. Maybe a week."

"But we have horses," John said.

Her gaze shot to his face. Horses? Did he mention that before?

"I can ride." She sat up straight. "If they're broke, I mean. They're broke, aren't they?"

"They are. That's not the problem." He turned his hat over in his hands. "The problem is, we used them as pack animals when we came here. Loaded as much as we could on them. To save as much as we could from the fire."

"I get it. You need them to pack stuff back up to the mountain," Laura said.

"Right."

"Could we make two trips?" Jeannie asked. "One to carry Laura, and another to get the rest of our things?"

A slight frown creased John's face.

"I think we might have to. It's not ideal. In fact, it's risky."

The porch creaked, and a moment later, someone knocked on the front door.

Laura froze.

Who could that be?

No one knew she was home, and no one knew the Andersons were staying here.

Her heart fluttered as she rose to her feet. Jeannie's face was ashen.

"No," John whispered. "I'll get it."

As he moved toward the door, his hand slid toward his holster.

"Danny. Come here!" Jeannie whispered and held her hands out to the child, who hustled toward her, a puzzled look on his face.

Laura stared at the door as John approached it.

"Who is it?" He called out.

"Jacob. Open up!"

Laura saw John's shoulders release their tension as he moved to unlock and open the door.

"C'mon in." He stood aside as a young man entered. Laura

guessed him to be early twenties. Tall and muscular, he wore a blue denim shirt much too warm for the hot July day, and camo pants with cargo pockets. Dusty black leather boots and a baseball cap completed his attire.

He swept off his hat as he stepped inside.

Danny freed himself from Jeannie's lap and raced toward the young man, launching himself into Jacob's arms.

Jacob caught him up effortlessly. "Hey, Danny! I've been looking for you."

The child grabbed Jacob's hat and put it on his own head, where it hung precariously.

John closed the door quickly, and turned to Laura.

"Have you met Jacob?"

"No." She moved toward the newcomer, smiling.

"Laura, I'd like you to meet Jacob Myers. Jacob, this is Laura. Josh and Willow's mom."

"I can see the resemblance." A wide smile made him winsomely handsome as he gripped her hand gently, chocolate eyes studying her own. His brown skin revealed time in the sun, and his dark hair was short but obviously growing out into uneven curls.

He'd make a perfect match for Raven.

She smiled as the thought caught her by surprise.

"Nice to meet you," she said. "Please, sit down."

She motioned toward the empty rocking chair, and returned to the sofa.

"Jacob was staying with Willow's group, before the fight and the fire," Jeannie said.

"The fight?" Laura's gaze spun from Jeannie to John. "What fight?"

"It's a long story, and we'll tell you all about it later, if that's okay." John's eyes turned to Jacob. "Have you decided? About Danny?"

Jacob settled into the rocking chair, the child nestling in his lap. He studied the kid. He didn't answer right away. Finally, he took a deep breath and heaved it out.

"I think I'll be keeping him."

Jeannie shifted in her seat. Laura looked at her. The older woman's face blanched, then frowned slightly.

"I've got a job, and I can feed us both." Jacob looked at John. "I don't know how you'd be able to take care of him. If the fire destroyed your place, your food stash –"

"I understand." The older man's voice was hoarse. His eyes shifted to his wife. She bit her lip and blinked hard. He looked back at Jacob.

"But who will watch him? While you're at work?"

"I had someone watching him."

"Not very well. He got away from you. Got lost. That's why we have him now," John countered.

Jacob stood up, the child wrapped around him like a monkey.

"Look, if I knew you could take care of him –" He looked helplessly from John to Jeannie. "If things were different... I'm sorry."

He walked to the door.

Jeannie sniffled.

"I'm really sorry." Jacob opened the door and let himself out, the child in his arms. He pulled the door closed behind him.

"Oh!" Tears slid from Jeannie's eyes. "I didn't get to say goodbye!"

She started toward the door. Her husband met her half way and wrapped his arms around her. She fell into them, sobs shaking her shoulders.

Laura lowered her head, feeling the woman's grief. Did Jeannie have children of her own? Grandchildren? Where were they now? Had she lost them?

Sympathy tears dampened her eyes.

Here she was, perhaps on the verge of getting her own children back, while Jeannie was losing the one child in her life. Yes, he'd only been with them a few days, but that was quite long enough to get attached to the little charmer.

She could only hope Danny would have a good life with Jacob.

25

I t was just sad. Laura swallowed the lump forming in her throat.

"Can't you do something?" Jeannie looked through her tears at her husband's face.

"I can't imagine what could be done." John stroked her hair, then placed a light kiss on her cheek. "If God wants us to have Danny, He will bring him back."

Jeannie leaned her head on her husband's chest and shut her eyes.

Laura got up and hobbled into the kitchen. They obviously needed a few minutes alone.

She found the rice Julie had cooked. In a covered pan on the propane stovetop, it was still hot. She got a fork and a bowl, and dished up a small amount.

The last thing she wanted was to hurl her food again.

She couldn't find any soy sauce, or even salt or pepper. It would be bland. Sitting at the table, she bowed her head and prayed for the food, and for Danny and John and Jeannie.

She took a tiny bite. It was the blandest food she'd ever tasted. But it was warm and it made her mouth water.

Slowly, she chewed the rice. It would be filling, and it was brown rice, so it'd be nourishing. That's what she needed to get well. And she needed to get well, so she could go to the mountains and find Willow and Josh.

John and Jeannie had told her about Willow's cabin. Laura tried to picture it in her mind. John said it was a pioneer cabin, at least a hundred years old. It had one room, with a half loft in the back where the boys slept. The girls slept on bunks under the loft. And the front of the cabin had a wood stove and a shelf or two, and a small table with two chairs.

She imagined sunshine streaming in the windows in the morning. The stove warming up the cabin during the coming winter.

If the little home hadn't burned in the forest fire.

She sighed heavily and took her bowl and fork to the sink.

Hopefully, God had protected her family's new home. As well as John and Jeannie's place. It sounded like they'd been good to the kids, sending over some food and stuff to help out.

Now she just needed to focus on getting well enough to travel. Rest and nourishment and antibiotics were just what the doctor ordered. She'd start with a nap.

THE NIGHT GREW cold and swept the smoke out of the front of the cave. Willow shivered and scooted deeper into her sleeping bag. Her throat was dry, but there was no more water.

They'd divided up the last of it before turning in for the night, with a tiny bit going to the chickens, the goats, and Gilligan. Josh and Matt had volunteered to go find more water, but Willow had nixed the idea because it she didn't think it was safe to walk out there yet.

Embers still glowed in the ashes on the ground.

The last thing they needed was to burn up the soles of their shoes and boots. Those were quickly becoming their most important possessions. And in the winter, they could mean the difference between life and death.

Willow turned over. Her hair reeked of smoke. She brushed it away from her face.

Couldn't wait to wash it.

In the morning, they'd head out while the air was still cold. They'd begin the hike to their cabin. And what would they find when they got there?

Would it still be standing?

Even if it was, the garden would have died from lack of water and the withering winds.

But they had to go back. What were their options?

Was there anywhere else to go?

Her mind tumbled with questions for hours. Finally, she slept fitfully and then awoke, groggy, as orange sunlight slanted though the cave's entrance.

Willow shivered. Mountain nights were cold, and felt even colder in the cave. She pulled on her boots and reached for her jacket and her Bible.

No one else was stirring yet. She bundled up her sleeping bag and took it to the entrance, where she wrapped it around her in the sunlight.

Her morning prayers were filled with praise for her group's survival through the fire, and petitions for their upcoming days. They would need God's help and grace, as they always did, but even more so now. Facing the loss of their garden and maybe their cabin, and preparing for winter – it was too much to handle on their own.

As she prayed, she looked out on the charred mountainside. It was strange how the fire had moved, running up some slopes and burning them out, while leaving some stands of timber almost unscathed, especially in the narrow draws. It looked like the fire had skipped over some areas.

There was less smoke today, at least here around the cave. That was good. It'd make their journey easier. She thanked God for that.

Sounds of people and animals awakening behind her led to the closing of her prayers. She stood and stretched, then rolled up her sleeping bag.

"Okay, people, let's get our stuff together and get going!"

As everyone got packed, Willow brushed Maria's hair and put on her little shoes.

The child chattered incessantly, much of it barely comprehensible, but Willow tried to answer her questions about Momma and breakfast. Finally, she helped the girl into her coat. By then, everyone else was ready to move out.

"Keep your eyes open. Watch for hotspots," Willow said. "Avoid damaging your shoes if you can."

She glanced at Maria.

"We'll need to carry her, but we can take turns."

Josh volunteered to take her for a while, and Maria happily held her arms up to him. Willow smiled. The half-siblings were quite a pair.

She led the group from the ledge in front of the cave, across the granite rocks to the burned forest. The sun warmed her head, but the cold air chilled her hands. It was good they were getting an early start.

It would be a long day.

LAURA WOKE WITH A STOMACH ACHE. She'd been sipping diluted colloidal silver before bedtime and once during the night when she woke up. That, on top of her tenuous digestive issues, gave her some distress.

She'd slept on her own bed, though, which was nice. At least she'd been comfortable. She sat up and checked her foot.

Maybe it looked a little better, or maybe she imagined that it did. In any case, it wasn't hurting as much. She poured some more colloidal silver on it and re-bandaged it, then went to the closet to find her hiking boots.

Like almost everything else in her house, the boots were missing. She hoped the kids had them. Otherwise, they'd been stolen by strangers.

Her barn boots were still there, though. And an old pair of running shoes.

Lots of her clothes were gone, but she found a pair of jeans and a black t-shirt, along with a couple of long-sleeved shirts and a sun hat. She dressed and brushed her hair, then found a belt to secure her now-oversized pants.

During her spring cleaning, she'd moved some winter items up to the attic. Maybe they were still there. Grabbing a flashlight she always kept in her nightstand, she went into the hall, pulled down the retractable steps, and climbed into the dark attic. The plastic bins looked undisturbed.

She brought them down into the hall and opened them. Hats, gloves, ski goggles, scarves, snowpants and two pairs of boots, plus a fleece jacket and an outer shell jacket. All good stuff!

Going back up, she found her old backpack, which she tossed down the steps, and a bin of her late husband's things, which she left there.

She dragged the totes into her bedroom, sorting the best items and packing them in the backpack. John had said they might leave today. He was antsy to get out of town, and Laura didn't blame him – she was, too.

Being the sick and injured one, she was the weak link. But she was strong and determined, and if they were ready to head out, she was ready to go with them.

She carried the backpack downstairs and found Jeannie in the kitchen.

"I made oatmeal, but there's also leftover rice." Jeannie gave her a shy smile.

"I'll stick with rice for now," Laura said. "My stomach is still kinda iffy from the colloidal silver."

"How are you feeling besides that?"

"Better. I slept a long time."

"Your color is better. How's your foot?"

"It doesn't hurt as much." Laura took a bowl of rice to the table. "I think it's on the mend."

"That's great!" Jeannie sat opposite her.

John came into the kitchen.

"Smells good! What are we having?"

"Oatmeal. It sticks to your ribs."

"Let's hope it does." He filled a bowl and came to the table. "How are you doing, Laura?"

"Good. Ready to go, if you are."

"You sure?" He stuck his spoon into his oatmeal and studied her. "Because we could go this morning. We'll adjust the packs and put you on one of the horses."

"I'm sure." Her heart swelled with the thought of seeing her family.

"Alright, then!" He stood up. "I'll go tell Mike and Julie."

"What about your breakfast?" Jeannie asked, frowning.

He scooped up the bowl and took it out the door with him. Jeannie shook her head.

"That man! When he gets his mind set on something –" She glanced at Laura. "You better get ready. I expect we'll be gone in less than an hour."

Just over thirty minutes later, Laura mounted one of the Andersons' horses, and the party headed out her driveway. She looked back over her shoulder at her home. The old white farmhouse on the small acreage with the little red barn out back – would she ever see it again?

It was alright if she didn't, as long as she found her kids. She pulled her sun hat low over her face and hoped nobody would recognize her. It was still early in the morning, but her neighbors were getting busy in their gardens before the heat of the day and the bees drove them away.

The sooner they got out of Ponderosa, the better.

WILLOW LED her group to a creek. She squatted in the ash on the bank and filtered water into her bottle, then took a sip.

"Ugh!" She glanced at Raven, who had just filled her own bottle. "It's warm!"

"And tastes gross!" Josh added.

Willow stared at the creek. The fire had heated the water, and also dropped burning trees in it, which heated it even more.

"We're just going to have to live with this," Willow said. "Maybe it'll be better tomorrow."

Gilligan lapped up a little water, then turned at stared at Raven.

"It's okay. Go ahead," she encouraged the dog.

Gilligan lapped again, then looked at Raven.

Matt laughed.

"I've never seen a dog look that confused before!"

"Poor guy." Raven rubbed Gilligan's ears. "It's okay, buddy."

Willow gathered her group and continued the hike. It should be possible to make it all the way to the cabin today, but it'd be a long, hard haul. Especially as the day got hotter. There wouldn't be much shade, since the fire had burned so many trees.

She marveled again about how some timber stands looked fine, while so much of the forest was decimated. It was like the fire was in such a hurry, it missed spots as it ran.

As they walked, the day grew hotter. And smokier.

When they crested a hilltop, Willow scanned the area. The fire had continued north, but appeared to turn east before it would have reached Ponderosa.

So the town was spared.

At least, from this particular blaze. She could see smoke rising from other, smaller fires, though.

And it was still July. Fire season was only beginning.

The temperatures kept rising as they hiked through the ash. It had to be 95 degrees, at least. The dry heat evaporated every bit of moisture, making Willow's skin feel scorched, her lips dehydrated, her nose burned.

If it were possible, her body and clothing would crackle as she walked. She was that hot and dry.

Around noon, they stopped for lunch under the shade of a stand of cedars that had survived the fire. The cedar grove provided a refreshing contrast to the burnt forest. Here, things were still green and shady. And much cooler.

They sat and finished off the rest of the food they'd brought with them. Willow looked at her friends and realized they wouldn't get back to the cabin today. Alan and Deborah appeared weary from the morning's hike, and everyone was hot and tired.

Willow sighed. She couldn't wait to get back to the cabin and see if it was still there.

But she'd have to. They could probably hike another couple hours later today, then finish the trek early in the morning. So she declared a siesta there in the shade.

"We'll rest here for a few hours, until it gets cooler. Then we'll hike again for a while, find a place to camp, and head home in the morning," she said.

"That sounds like a good plan." Clark's voice was solemn. "We don't want anyone getting heat stroke."

Tʜᴇ ᴅᴀʏ's heat had finally given way to cool evening temperatures, and Laura's whole body ached by the time she and her new friends reached John Anderson's driveway. The blackened landscape stole her breath.

A sooty foundation told her where their house had stood. Twisted metal indicated the barn's location. The fire had taken everything.

She climbed off her mare and hobbled to Jeannie, whose mouth gaped as she stared at her home. Or where it had been, until this week.

"I am so sorry." Laura swallowed. She wrapped an arm around the older lady.

John stood a few feet ahead of them, silent.

What was there to say? It was gone.

Everything was gone.

She'd been told her own children lived not too far away. Did their cabin look like this?

———

26

It was a long time before anyone spoke. Finally, John cleared his throat. Then he turned toward them, his face a mix of pain and determination.

"We need to find a place to spend the night."

"I have an idea." Julie, the quiet one, spoke up. "What about the house down the road? The one where we had the fight? It was vacant when we left."

"The owners might have come home," Jeannie said through sniffles.

"Probably not. I'd been feeding and watering the rabbits there after the fight until we evacuated, and no one ever showed up." John rubbed his chin. "It's a good idea, Julie. And it's not far. We can be there before dark."

Laura pulled herself up on the blue roan mare, and John led the way back down the dusty Forest Service road as dusk deepened. The fire hadn't burned this area. It was apparently just outside the path of the fire. Here, nothing was affected, while the Andersons had lost everything less than a quarter mile away.

John started in a driveway, then stopped.

"You ladies wait here with the animals," he said quietly. "I'll go in with Mike. Even if the owners never returned, there might be squatters here by now."

The men moved into the darkness, and Laura prayed with Jeannie and Julie. Finally, they returned.

"It's good," John said. "Let's put the animals in the barn."

They came into a clearing with a two-story older home and a neat yard. Behind it, a small creek ran past a garden and beyond that, Laura could see a barn. She turned the mare toward it, and dismounted outside.

"I'll take care of the horses," Julie said, taking the reins from her. "You go inside and take care of your foot."

The house was dark, but Jeannie had already found and lit an old oil lamp. In the living room, Laura noticed some blood stains on a chair and a rug, but otherwise, the house appeared to be in good shape. There was a master bedroom on the first floor, and upstairs there were three tiny bedrooms and a bathroom.

Laura took off her boots, cleaned and dressed her wound, and dropped onto a bed. She'd barely closed her eyes before she was enveloped in sleep.

WILLOW WOKE early and sneezed the dusty smoke from her lungs. Everything was gritty from the ash, like it had been after the volcanic eruption. Her eyes itched, but she didn't dare rub them. Her fingers would smear irritants into her eyes, making it worse.

They'd slept under a canopy of intact cedars, which kept them out of the heavy ash, but also made the morning air feel colder.

If anyone hadn't been awake already, her sneezing woke them up.

"Bless you!" Raven said, sitting up in her sleeping bag.

"Thanks." Willow sneezed one more time. Her eyes watered and her nose ran. What she'd give for a paper tissue!

"Let's get up early and hit the trail before it gets hot," Raven suggested.

"Amen to that!" Willow nudged her brother, who burrowed deeper into his sleeping bag. "You'll be glad, later."

This was met with a muffled groan.

"Get up, or you get the water treatment!" She nudged him with her foot.

He growled his displeasure, but then stuck his head out.

"One of these days, I'll –"

"You'll what?" She laughed and tousled his too-long hair. "Get up, sleepyhead! Let's go!"

Jaci and Clark got their family ready, while Willow took Maria to wash up at the stream. The water was cooler today. Alan and Deborah came down to fill their water bottles.

"Just a few hours, and we'll be back at the cabin!" Willow dried her hands on her jeans.

"I hope it survived. If it didn't..." Deborah let the sentence trail off, then glanced at her husband. "God has a plan."

"That's right." He took her hand. "Let's go find out what it is."

The group gathered for prayer before they began the final trek back to the cabin site. Willow's stomach turned with hunger and apprehension, but when they prayed, it settled. It would not be long before they had an answer about their home.

She led the group as briskly as she dared, considering that not everyone was in early adulthood like she was. If it had just been her and Raven, they would have run. But they had grandparents with them, and little Maria, and everything took longer.

The sun rose higher and began to heat the hills as they got close to home. They trudged through ash, climbed over blackened, fallen trees, and tried to not slip on sooty rocks.

Finally, there was only one hill to climb, and they'd have their answer.

Willow's heart raced. Her mouth dried. She scurried up the hill.

But she could not see the cabin!

Because live trees were blocking the view!

The fire had not consumed the bowl-shaped area they called home. At least, not this part of it. So there was a very good chance the cabin was still standing.

She and Raven whooped and cheered, and the others joined in when they saw what she was looking at.

"Almost there, guys! Let's go!" She started down the slope through the trees, and would have broken into a run if she hadn't been carrying a crate of chickens.

Finally, they reached the clearing. And there, in all its pioneer glory, stood the old weathered cabin, the sun highlighting its chinked logs.

Willow fell on her knees right there and cried.

And thanked God.

Then she got up, hugged her brother and Raven, and led the group home.

The garden would be gone, she knew. Without water, the tender plants would have mostly shriveled up and died. Still, somehow, they'd find a way to survive. God had a plan.

"We'll need to dig up everything from the trench," she said. "And water the animals. And the garden, if any of the plants made it."

As they approached, though, she thought she saw a vision.

Or a mirage.

The garden flourished. The plants stood tall and green. Nothing was browned or withered.

She blinked, then rubbed her grimy eyes. They watered. She blinked again. The garden looked great!

Willow dropped her crate of chickens, sending them into a squawking fit, and ran to the garden. The plants were healthy. Not one of them drooped from dehydration.

How could that be?

She looked around, puzzled.

Had it rained? Just here?

Dust blew across the ground in front of the barn. There had been no rain.

She got close and looked the soil. The rows had been watered. Someone had watered their garden!

But who? And were they still here? In her cabin, perhaps?

LAURA AND JOHN mounted the two horses. He'd promised to take her to the cabin first thing this morning. Today was the day! To see her kids! To hug them and kiss them and look at their beautiful faces.

They left the barnyard and started out the driveway.

"Thank you, John. I know you've got a lot on your mind." She relaxed in the saddle, her hips absorbing the mare's motion.

"My questions have been answered. Yours are still out there."

It was true. Sad as it was, he knew what happened to his home. She didn't know what happened to her kids or their home. Hopefully, they'd find out in an hour or two.

"Last night, you mentioned rabbits at the vacant house. Did they survive?" She asked.

"Yeah." John glanced at her. "I gave them food and tons of water before we evacuated, and they all made it except one bunny. They were happy to get fresh water last night!"

"Oh, that's good."

She cringed as they reached the area that had been burned,

then turned up John's driveway. It looked like a black charcoal sketch, full of soot and destruction.

"If you don't mind waiting a minute, I need to check something." John swung out of his saddle.

"That's fine." She pulled on the reins and her mare came to a stop.

John led his gelding up a slope behind the charred foundation. With gloved hands, he swept away ash and soot, and a metal door appeared in the hillside. Laura stared. Did he have a mine back there? A bomb shelter?

He yanked the door open, and went inside. Moments later, he emerged, smiling. He mounted up and returned to where she waited.

"That's our root cellar. Actually, it's an old mine shaft that we converted. There are old mines all over the place in Montana's mountains," he explained. "From the glory days. Gold, silver, copper, whatever."

Laura was dying of curiosity. She tried to be polite, but failed.

"So? What's in there?"

"Lots of stuff." John started his horse up the hill, and Laura fell in beside him. "When we thought we might have to evacuate, we crammed that thing full. Food and supplies. I didn't know whether it could survive a fire like that, but it did, praise God!"

"Wow." Laura pondered it. John and his family would be okay. They had a house to live in for now, and supplies to get them through the winter.

She smiled. "That's great, John."

He nodded and grinned.

"I wanted to check it last night, but it was nearly dark and we were all so tired. Plus, the shock of finding the house like that... I didn't think we could bear it if we'd found the supplies destroyed, too. That's why I waited until this morning."

He smiled, then urged his horse forward. Laura touched her heels to her mare's flanks, and they trotted up the hill.

Soon, she would get her own answers.

WILLOW LOOKED AT THE CABIN. Was someone in there? Maybe watching them now? Maybe with guns trained on her and her friends?

Her muscles tensed. She glanced at her friends, who'd gathered around to marvel at the garden.

"Guys! Someone watered these plants!" She spoke in a whisper. "What if they're in the cabin now?"

Alan's hand moved toward his holster.

"You all take cover," he ordered. "I'll check it out."

"I'm coming with you," Willow said, reaching for her Smith & Wesson.

As their group scattered into the trees, she and Alan moved quickly to the cabin's door. He took a position near the window, and she tapped on the doorpost.

"Anybody inside?" She called.

There was no response. She gripped the handle and glanced at Alan. He nodded his readiness.

She pushed the door open and paused, but there was still no response. She stepped in quickly, moving to the side so Alan could follow her.

A moment passed as her eyes adjusted to the dim light.

At first, she saw no one. Then, she noticed a person lying on a lower bunk in the back. She hurried forward. The man didn't move.

Was he dead?

As Willow got closer, she recognized him.

"Uncle Tony!" She spoke loudly, partly from surprise.

He still didn't move. She remembered his heart condition. Had he had a heart attack?

"Tony!" She shook his shoulder.

"Wha – Huh?" Weary blue eyes blinked open. He lifted his head, then dropped it back on the mattress. "Oh. You're back. Finally."

"You watered the garden," Willow said.

"Where's Raven?" His eyes scanned the cabin for her.

"She's outside."

"She's okay?"

"Yes, she's fine." Willow squatted next to the bed.

"Good. I couldn't let the garden fail. She might have starved. I had to take care of my little bird." Tony closed his eyes. "If you don't mind, I'm gonna nap. I'm tired."

"Of course." Willow stood, smiling. "Thank you, Tony. We all might have starved."

Tony faked a snore, and Willow and Alan went outside, closing the door gently behind them. Willow beckoned an "all clear" to the forest, and her friends emerged. Gathering in the shade, she explained that Raven's uncle had watered the garden, and he was napping and not to be disturbed.

Besides, they had plenty to do outside: haul more water, take care of the animals, and dig up their belongings from the trench where they'd buried them days ago.

Willow decided she and Josh should take first shift digging, since it was the hottest and dirtiest work. Everyone else picked a project and got started. Beth had the easiest job, watching Maria under the shade of the tall pines. Willow watched them and smiled. It was good to be young.

Gilligan's ears rose and he stared toward the forest, sniffing, his body erect and muscles tense. He let out a low woof, then a full bark. Then another bark.

What was his deal?

Willow stopped shoveling. Was it a predator? A person?

A horse and rider entered the clearing, waving. And another one, right behind them. The first was a man, the second a woman.

Willow recognized the horses. They belonged to the Andersons. And John was on the big bay gelding. But that was not Jeannie on the blue roan mare.

It looked like – she looked like – Willow shaded her eyes against the hot July sun. It looked like her mom.

If only it was! If only it could be!

Tears touched her eyes as she felt such longing. She swallowed.

The woman waved wildly, and urged her horse into a run.

Straight for Willow and Josh.

And it looked like her mom, looked so much like her mom!

Then she was there, swinging off the mare as she pulled it to a stop.

It was her mom!

But how?

Even as she was nearly bowled over in an embrace, she couldn't believe it. Was this real? Surely it was a dream!

Mom was so skinny!

Josh grabbed them both in a tight group hug.

This was a dream. A wonderful, happy dream. She didn't want to wake up!

It felt real.

Willow pulled back enough to stare at her mom's face. Sunburned and thin, but definitely her mother's face.

"Don't let me wake up!" She said it aloud, fearfully.

"I love you so much!" Mom planted a kiss on her cheek, then one on Josh. "Both of you!"

And Willow didn't wake up.

She was awake!

"This is amazing. How?" She stared at her mom, afraid if she stopped looking at her, she'd disappear again.

"Long story. I'll tell you all about it later." She ruffled Josh's hair. "You need a haircut, young man!"

Josh pulled out of her embrace, glancing shyly toward Beth and Delia.

John gathered the reins of the mare Mom had been riding. A huge grin lit his face as he watched them. Willow looked around. Her friends had gathered.

"Everybody, this is Mom!" She grinned. "Mom, this is everybody!"

Willow's heart filled and overflowed with joy. Real introductions and all the stories would come later. For now, she had her mom. And for now, that was all she wanted.

The End.

"Are we gonna have dinner tonight?" Danny turned his little brown face up toward Jacob's, his dark eyes filled with a sad mix of hope and grief that shouldn't be seen in a child so young.

"Yes, you'll have dinner." Jacob wasn't certain whether he himself would eat, but the boy would.

Danny slipped his hand in Jacob's as they walked toward Heidi's neighborhood.

"I'm hungry now."

The child's hand felt bony and cold. His face was thinner now than a month ago. He'd been losing weight, when he needed to be gaining it.

Without thinking, Jacob pulled a small boiled potato from his pocket.

"Here." He handed it to the boy.

Danny bit into the potato, eating it like an apple as they turned onto Heidi's street.

A cool wind signaled the approaching autumn as Jacob turned to look at Willow's Wilderness. The Christians up there must be in a scramble to prepare for winter. They'd need to be getting firewood, and harvesting as much food and wild game as possible.

It'd be a lean winter, for sure. The wildfires had no doubt destroyed much of the wildlife, as well as most of the habitat. And the forests were still burning, destroying and smoking up the whole region.

Soon, the fall rains would come and tamp down the fires. Winter would put them totally out. But devastation would remain where they'd chewed through the forest, and it'd take decades to restore it all.

Decades? Jacob frowned. Was there that much time left?

Not according to his adoptive parents. As Christians, they'd been convinced that the end of the world was imminent.

And Jacob was beginning to think they were right. Maybe.

A trio of teenage boys approached. All three stared at Danny. And his half-eaten potato.

Idiot! Jacob cursed his stupidity. What had possessed him to give Danny a morsel of food in broad daylight? In public!

Instinctively, he rested his right hand on his Glock, and pulled Danny closer with his left hand.

"Heads up!" He hissed.

Danny looked up and dropped his potato when he saw the teens, one of whom swung a baseball bat as he swaggered toward them. Danny bent to pick up the vegetable.

"Leave it there," Jacob ordered, gripping the child's hand firmly.

He stared at the teens, who alternately watched his gun hand and glanced at the potato. He didn't want to kill anybody, but these kids were starving and desperate. If they forced a confrontation, he'd make it lethal.

"We are going to cross the street," Jacob announced as he pulled his Glock from his holster. "If any of you follow us, I'll shoot you."

Gripping Danny's hand tightly, he stared at the ravenous teenagers. Not taking his eyes off them, he turned Danny into the street and began to cross it.

The moment after he stepped away from the fallen food, the teens moved in like hyenas in a mad scramble for the half-eaten potato.

Jacob hustled Danny across the street, then holstered his handgun and scooped up the kid. While the teens were distracted with their fight over the food, Jacob turned, sprinted around the corner, and raced into the alley that ran behind Heidi's house.

They were only two blocks away. At the end of the first block, Jacob slowed and glanced back. No one was following, as far as he could tell.

He hurried to Heidi's back yard and set Danny down. Pushing the gate open, he softly announced his arrival – hoping it was loud enough that she'd hear, but the local hoodlums wouldn't.

He closed the gate and rushed Danny to the back door.

Heidi answered it as soon as he knocked.

"You should put a padlock on your alley gate," he said, pushing Danny inside. "Who knows who might come through there."

"Why'd you come that way?" She smoothed her short black dress. Other than ruby red lipstick, she didn't appear to be wearing any makeup. Her blue eyes looked dull and tired.

"Ran into some trouble."

"What kind of trouble?" Marcus came from the living room and stood in the kitchen entryway. "Do I need to bash some heads?"

"Hungry teenagers." Jacob handed his remaining potato to Danny. "Here's your dinner. Why don't you go play upstairs?"

Marcus stared accusingly at Jacob. "Hungry? How'd they know you had food?"

"I gave Danny a little potato."

The police captain's face turned red. "You did WHAT? Are you crazy, or just plain stupid?"

Jacob let him fume a moment before he answered.

"I had my mind on something else."

"Like what? A woman?" Marcus smirked.

Jacob's gaze shot toward Heidi. Averting her eyes, she put a dirty glass in the sink and brushed past him, disappearing down the hall.

"It doesn't matter. It won't happen again."

"It better not. You could get killed! You could get us all killed!" Marcus crossed his arms.

Unlike the rest of Ponderosa's population, Marcus didn't seem to be losing any weight. And Heidi's slim figure looked exactly the same as it did a month ago. They were eating just fine. Meanwhile, many residents were starving, like the feral teenagers down the street. And others were headed that way, like Jacob and Danny.

Which reminded Jacob... he needed to talk to Marcus about his pay.

Marcus unfolded his arms and sauntered back to the living room. Jacob followed.

"We need to re-negotiate my salary," Jacob said. "I'm losing weight, and so is Danny."

"You and the rest of the country," Marcus growled. "Nobody's getting fat around here!"

"It's getting more dangerous out at the farm," Jacob persisted. "I can't keep working for wages that are going to leave us starving this winter."

"So. You want to quit and starve now?"

"We need more calories. Look at the kid, he's getting skinnier every day!"

"He looks fine." Marcus dropped into the recliner and stared at the carpet. "But speaking of Danny, we need to get him chipped."

"What?" Jacob couldn't believe his ears. "What on earth for?"

"It's the law. All students have to be chipped before the first day of school."

"There is no school. You think teachers are gonna show up and not get paid? Besides, there are no functional chip readers, since the EMP fried everything."

"All I know is, next week is September, and the teachers better show up."

Jacob shook his head in disbelief.

"They won't. Plus, Danny is only four. Nobody has to be chipped until they turn six."

Marcus turned his dark eyes toward Jacob.

"Age six, or when they start school. Danny will be in kindergarten." He raised his hand as if to ward off Jacob's protest. "We've got the supplies at the station. Bring him down tomorrow, and we'll get it done. Then you won't have to worry about it later."

Jacob stared at Marcus. This was craziness. Who cared if anyone had the ID chip anymore? They didn't work. And they wouldn't, until everything was fixed from the EMP.

"I don't understand why you're even bringing this up." Jacob took a deep breath. "It has nothing to do with anything. There's literally no point in chipping anyone. The stupid things are useless!"

"Because it's the LAW!" Marcus thundered. He rose angrily from his chair and moved toward Jacob. "Besides, if it doesn't matter, why NOT get it done?"

He eyeballed Jacob suspiciously. "Unless you're opposed to the chip? Maybe you don't have the I.D. yourself?"

He reached for Jacob's right hand, but Jacob sidestepped.

"Don't be ridiculous!" He shoved his hands in his pockets.

~

Willow Archer took a break from filleting the trout. She stretched and yawned. August had been a hot, hard month, and she was looking forward to September, which would bring cooler temperatures and maybe some rain.

She was sick of breathing smoke.

On the bench in front of her lay three more trout for dinner. The rest were to be smoked and put away in the cache for this winter.

Raven's Uncle Tony had promised to teach them how to properly smoke the fish so the meat would remain edible. He'd already done a lot – teaching the group about better hunting techniques and how to make jerky. He'd also helped them build the cache, a tiny cabin on tall stilts designed to keep food away from bears and other marauders.

Across the clearing, she watched Matt and Josh chopping logs into firewood. With axes, it was a slow, tedious process.

Raven, Mom, Deborah and Jaci worked in the garden with the teen girls, weeding and harvesting. Nights were getting colder now, and soon they'd have a hard freeze. The short growing season was one of Montana's big survival obstacles.

Well, that and the winter, obviously. And the constant struggle for food.

She glanced at Maria, playing with Gilligan and a couple of pine cones. Everyone made sure the adorable toddler ate well, even when the rest of the group went to bed hungry. Since Candy had died, Maria had been adopted by everybody. And

Willow still hadn't revealed the fact they were half-sisters. How would Mom take it? It could be devastating.

She turned her attention back to the fish. Soon, Alan and Clark would return from the new family's cabin, where Uncle Tony was helping them finish the roof. If they couldn't find, fabricate, or scavenge a stove, they'd have to build a fireplace before winter. Other than that, it was habitable now.

A sharp bark from Gilligan turned her attention to where he was looking – the far side of the clearing.

A rider on a big bay horse stepped out of the forest, and the man waved his hat until Willow raised her arm in a welcoming wave.

John Anderson was coming to see them!

He probably wouldn't make the trip over here unless he had a real reason. She hoped it was good news. Or at least not bad news.

The last time she'd seen John was the week after Mom arrived. Willow's group had volunteered to help John and Jeannie move all the gear that had survived the fire in their mine/root cellar to their new place down the road. In return, the Andersons had given them two breeding pairs of rabbits, which now resided in their little shed-turned-barn.

John rode up to her. His gelding tossed his head and snorted at Gilligan.

"Hi," Willow said, watching John's face for any indication of concern or worry. She saw none.

"Hey, there." John dismounted and patted the bay's neck. "How are you guys doing?"

"Okay, I guess." Willow's friends began to gather around them. "Just getting ready for winter. How about you?"

"The same." He shook hands with the group. "That's why I'm here, actually."

He fixed her with a gaze.

"I've got two chainsaws, with extra chains and tools to sharpen them, but no gas or oil."

Wow, that was a bummer. Getting wood in for the winter was a huge project, and having a functional chainsaw would reduce the work and time by ninety percent, probably. She frowned slightly.

"I'm sorry we can't help. We don't have any oil or gas, either."

"I didn't expect you would, but I still think you can help." John glanced around the group. "I believe there are several vacant homes down near the highway, and if we could take a team to scavenge, I'd share whatever we collect, plus give one chainsaw to you."

Josh grinned.

"Yes!" He looked at Matt, who exchanged a fist-bump with him.

"We're in!" Matt agreed.

"Not so fast." Willow narrowed her eyes at her brother. "That will be real dangerous. Someone might be home in what you think is a vacant house. Or squatters might have moved in. Or you could meet trouble on the road. Any of those situations could result in a shoot-out."

John nodded.

"That's why we need a team, instead of just me and my three. More eyes and ears, for one thing."

"And more guns, if something goes wrong," Willow added. She shook her head. "I'd hate to lose anyone over a chainsaw. We have axes. We'll get by."

"You're not the one chopping," Josh argued.

"And I'm not saying prayers at your funeral," she shot back. She focused a meaningful look at their mother. "Some help, please?"

Laura sighed as she looked from her son to her daughter.

"I can see both sides. Who knows? You might actually come

across some good gear, or even food, in one of those houses." Lines crossed her forehead as she frowned. "Or, you might get shot. I'd be inclined to vote no."

"Thanks, I think," Willow said, rolling her eyes. She turned to John. "Obviously, our group will need to discuss this and pray about it."

"No problem. I expected as much." He glanced around the group. "You all sort this out and let me know. You know where to find us."

"Sounds good," Willow said.

"If you're in, why don't you come by tomorrow morning, early. If I don't see you, I'll know you chose not to participate."

He shook her hand, swung into the saddle, and tipped his hat to the group before trotting back the way he'd arrived.

My newsletter readers will be notified when my next novel is ready. My free newsletter goes out about once a month. It includes updates, discounts, and freebies and giveaways.

You can sign up at
www.JamieLeeGrey.com

LETTER TO READERS

Dear new friends,

Thank you for choosing this series. I hope you enjoyed it. Would you do me a favor and write a quick review on the site where you bought it? It will help me as an author, and it will help your fellow readers decide whether this book is for them. **Thank you very much!**

If you'd like to communicate with me, you can contact me at my website, JamieLeeGrey.com

May God's face shine upon you and bring you peace.

All the best,

Jamie Lee Grey

ACKNOWLEDGMENTS

Readers and friends – Thank you for reading, and for your support. You make it worthwhile. Special thanks go to my beta readers for encouragement and feedback, especially Deb, who has been a huge help this year.

Candle Sutton – For the past decade, Candle has been my amazing critique partner. She's also become a true friend and partner in prayer. (Hey, everybody, be sure to check out Candle's books at www.CandleSutton.com .)

My husband – You are the best. Thank you for your encouragement and support of this project, and all my other crazy ideas.

Jesus Christ – My life and breath, and the giver of all good gifts. Thank You.

BOOKS BY JAMIE LEE GREY

Holy War

Band of Believers series

Book 1: Dissent

Book 2: Duplicity

Book 3: Destruction

Book 4: Darkness

Daughter of Babylon series

Book 1: California

Book 2: New York

Book 3: America

Book 4: Oregon

Made in United States
Orlando, FL
27 September 2024

51988674R10153